A Most

Unsuitable Lover

A Most

Unsuitable Lover

KELSEY SWANSON

Author's Note

This book is intended to be a standalone novel, but it does take place after the trio of books in "The Stratford Family" series; Ian makes appearances in books two and three. You shouldn't have an issue enjoying this story if you haven't read them, but it is recommended you do so to fully appreciate Ian's backstory. You can find <u>The Baron's Folly</u>, <u>Saving the Viscount</u>, and <u>Loving Mister Stratford</u> on Amazon!

For every childhood stolen by illness, and those who refuse to allow it to define them.

Chapter One

London, August of 1826

Doctor Ian McCullom narrowly dodged a messenger boy as he careened recklessly through the bustling walkway, heedless of those around him and bent only on earning an extra penny or two if he delivered his note with due haste. He shook his head and righted his beaver hat before resuming his pace. The early afternoon was surprisingly clear and crisp for an August day. The soot in the air was less cloying and summer's heat loosened its grip upon London. The Season had wound down some weeks earlier, but, rather than retreat to their country estates as he'd hoped, the English elite seemed bent upon staying within the City for the time being…which placed them squarely within Ian's jurisdiction. After the months of unending calls and social events, emergencies and overwrought alarmists, Ian had so been looking forward to a moment to catch his breath.

He paused at the edge of the narrow walkway and attempted to gauge when it might be safe to cross to his destination. It seemed as if the whole of London had taken to the break in the heat and the clarity of the air to fill the streets around him. Unfortunately, the scents of horseflesh and unwashed bodies smothered any hint of fresh air he might have hoped for during his outing. The cacophony of peddlers and coachmen, liveried tigers and roughly-dressed cart drivers all squawked for supremacy in the din which seemed to reverberate all the more thanks to the height of the fashionable buildings lining the street in their orderly rows of shops and cafes.

The door to the business behind him swung open and a wave of flour-scented air wafted into the street, momentarily masking the otherwise unpleasant odors. He knew the bakery well and sometimes sent his housekeeper there to purchase bread. The shop was the only one he'd found that could closely enough replicate the crusty bread of his youth and afford him that slight bit of nostalgic escape.

The brief reprieve on the air was all-too-quickly whisked away on the haunches of the next lathered steed which rumbled past.

As he continued to monitor the traffic and wait for an unlikely opening to cross, the lyrical tones of a woman behind him cut through the din like a songbird in a forest of crows. She must have been the patron who exited the bakery, as she was busy gently instructing her young, gangly footman to take care with the parcel of baked goods. Ian saw out of the corner of his eye a lavender skirt shot with iridescent threads as the woman finally came even with him. She stood slightly more than an arm's distance away as she also seemed to be watching the bustle on the street—perhaps awaiting her driver or preparing to cross as he was.

Ian's gaze sidelong traveled higher to take in the fashionable cut of her sleeves, the amethyst gems winking in her dainty earlobes, and the rich, inky curls caressing her ivory neck. He caught only a glimpse of her profile—a pert nose and daintily sculpted chin—as she glanced from side to side.

What little he saw was evidence of a pretty young woman; well-born and English in the way she dressed and the manner with which she held herself. As someone who was not of this heritage, Ian had spent a great deal of time examining such mannerisms to fit in and be better accepted within broader, more well-off social circles. No matter how the English liked to think themselves forward-thinking, there remained a decidedly prejudicial undercurrent when they were confronted with a man born and bred with the blood of the Scottish Highlands.

Just then, the young woman turned fully in his direction and Ian's lungs forgot their duty. She initially looked past him with a pair of the brightest blue eyes he'd ever seen. Rimmed with long, coal-colored lashes, her eyes were striking against the pale flesh of her cheeks and the contrasting darkness of her hair.

That captivating gaze flicked back over him like a butterfly and rested upon his face. Their eyes met and a spark jumped deep inside of Ian's chest. It was a primal, irrational moment where the male in him recognized a desirable female. And by God, this woman was lovely…and utterly unattainable.

Still, their eyes inexplicably held.

Even as there was a shout from behind the woman, they remained frozen in that languorous moment…right up until another messenger boy burst through the crowd up the street, dodged between two affronted women, narrowly spun free of the grasp of a man who attempted to cuff the lad for his reckless behavior, and then knocked straight into the young woman in lavender.

Her eyes widened a moment before her lips parted in shock. Her arms swung in a wild windmill in a futile attempt to remain upright.

The messenger boy dashed onward and was once more swallowed by the crowd.

Ian watched as the woman tilted precariously forward and into the path of the traffic where she would undoubtedly be trampled and seriously injured—if not permanently maimed or killed.

Ian cursed and dropped the paper-wrapped parcel he'd been carrying as he lunged forward to snatch her wrist not a moment too soon. He yanked the woman back to the safety of the walkway, but their collective weight collided with the sizable frame of her footman. Together, they all tumbled to the ground in an ungraceful spectacle. The young woman yelped against his chest as he landed with a thud. His beaver hat tumbled from his head and rolled into the street. Ian watched with more than mild annoyance as it was quickly flattened beyond all recognition beneath the muddy hooves of a fruitmonger's mule.

That damned hat had been expensive, too.

Looking down at the dark curls pressed against his chest, he took quick stock of himself and realized there were no immediate injuries other than a likely bruise to his arse. He heard the footman groan and shuffle to his feet before attempting to gather up his packages before they could be further damaged or snatched up by greedy fingers.

There were murmurs of spectators surrounding them and Ian knew they needed to stand and he had to unhand her before much more was made of the scene.

"Are you alright, miss? Are you injured?" he asked gently, his heart pounding in his chest. It had been a dangerously near miss. He gripped her upper arms in his hands and, though he could feel the fragility of the petite bones beneath his practiced fingers, there was a strength to her frame that was surprising. Her dark curls bounced as she nodded her head and turned to look up into his face.

"I—I believe so. Thank you, sir."

Ian was struck once more by the color of her eyes. This close, however, he could see they were rimmed in the darkest of blues; the color of far-off mountains in the hazy early morning light.

"My lady!" the footman clad in black-and-yellow livery rushed over, abandoning his task of gathering up the parcels once he saw his employer sprawled on the ground in a pool of purple skirts. The lad's fretting grew until the woman in Ian's arms reassured him.

"I'm well, Thomas. Here; please take my hand and help me to my feet before people begin to believe I'm just another fixture to be trod upon." The footman assisted her and Ian's legs were free of her slight weight. "There now—oh!" She stumbled as she attempted to put weight upon her right ankle.

Ian saw her grimace and lurched to stand and catch her about her slim waist before she crumpled to the ground once more.

"It would appear that I'm not so well as I believed," she laughed breathily, and Ian found her attempt at levity quite charming. His tongue felt suddenly too large for his mouth as she met his gaze once more.

"You're clearly injured," he said, forcing the words from his mouth. "Your ankle must be examined to be sure there is no break." Ian gestured as he helped her stay upright. "I am a physician. My offices are just across the street two blocks away; please, allow me to make sure it is not serious."

"I couldn't impose," the young woman began as she gave her head a little shake. A few more curls had come loose from her coiffure and fell to her temples to dance as she moved.

"Nonsense. It is no imposition at all. In fact, I insist we have a look at that ankle." Ian leaned in closer and lowered his voice. "Besides, we're making much more of a scene just standing here. If we retreat to my offices, it will allow you to compose yourself in more privacy." This seemed to speak to her rational side and she finally nodded in assent. She, too, must have felt the many pairs of eyes upon them as she was propped up in the middle of the walkway on a busy afternoon.

"Thomas, please gather the parcels," she said to the footman; "We will be retreating before I become even more of an object of interest." Ian readily accepted the brunt of her slight weight and helped her balance as the footman stooped to gather what parcels he could.

"Would mind retrieving mine as well?" Ian asked, tipping his chin in the direction of his discarded box, half surprised that someone hadn't already snagged it and run off. The footman obliged and, together, all three of them set off for Ian's offices.

*****

Juliette leaned on the wrought iron railing of the neat Townhouse set just off of the busy street of shops on which she'd nearly lost her life. She watched her savior's broad shoulders clad in a simple black overcoat now scuffed and dusty from landing on the walkway and absorbing the full brunt of their fall.

"Should we be doing this, my lady?" Thomas hissed, eyes wide like those of a cornered mouse—an oddly juxtaposing expression on a young man who stood at more than six feet in height. "Surely His Lordship would prefer I escort you home and send for his physician." She could hear the young man's nerves in his uneven tone.

"Don't worry so; the man is obviously a physician," Juliette attempted to reassure him as she gestured to the carved and painted sign above the door announcing to all the profession of the man who dwelled inside. Despite this, the poor footman continued to fret, glancing around as if he were afraid of being caught committing some heinous crime. To be fair, Juliette couldn't blame him over much. Thomas had only recently been promoted to the role of footman and he was probably terrified of losing his position for inadvertently allowing his mistress into a dangerous situation. Not to mention, Juliette knew her brother's temper could make even grown men quake in their boots and scramble for cover.

"But, my lady…" the footman whimpered.

"It'll be alright," Juliette sighed and patted his shoulder. She turned her attention away from her anxious servant and back to the large form of the man before them. He wore well-made, if simple, clothing. The coat hugged his broad shoulders with a finesse which spoke of a fine tailor. The blue twine encasing the paper-wrapped package he once more held beneath his arm was the trademark of a well-known bookstore and lending library in the West End. This was a man who was well-off enough to dress in tailored clothing of good quality, but not so rich as to retain staff to carry and deliver his packages for him; or open the door to his residence when he was not in attendance.

He wore his longish hair in a neat queue at the nape of his neck. Now that she was able to get a good look at him without his ill-fated beaver hat, she noticed his hair was not brown, but a rich auburn chestnut which shone with threads of dark gold in the afternoon sunlight. How interesting. The man replaced his key in his pocket as the door swung open. He turned to the side to allow Juliette to enter first.

"After you, My Lady," he said. And not for the first time did she enjoy the rich, velvety burr to his speech. His diction was impeccable, but no amount of practice could ever completely erase the lolling Scottish tint to his tone—not to her practiced ears. She returned his small smile with gratitude and placed her hand in his so he might help her over the threshold. They were admitted to a pleasantly appointed foyer with an ivory-tiled floor and walls papered in a simple green stripe. It was clean and the scent of citrus lingered in the air, along with a hint of something Juliette could not name. Something herbal and warm and pleasant.

Their host set his parcel on a spindle-legged oaken side table. "My offices are belowstairs," he explained. "I felt, in your condition, that the extra distance through the alleyway to that entrance might be a burden. Come." He gestured for Thomas to help her down the hallway to a door and set of stairs. With his assistance, Juliette was able to maneuver down the steps and into what she could only assume had once been the kitchens and other servants' quarters for the Townhouse. Her experience with the lower level of dwellings was extremely limited, but she doubted highly that the rooms of this home were typical.

Similar to what little she'd seen of the main floor, these basement rooms were immaculately clean and well-appointed in a simple, welcoming manner. The muted yellow-papered walls and black-and-white checkered tiles decorated what she assumed must have been a sitting room of sorts, lined as it was with a trio of simple wooden chairs. Off to one side was an open doorway leading to what remained of the kitchens, as well as another door butting up to the back alley. This must have been the aforementioned entrance through which the physician's patients usually came. The secondary basement foyer created a hallway that led to yet another door; this one was polished mahogany. It was to this door that the physician escorted Juliette and her footman. He closed the distance in only two long strides and held the door open to admit them.

Once she entered, a wave of that warm herbal scent washed over her. Glancing around in interest, she realized from where it had originated. A wall of small pigeonhole cubbies stretched up from a long desk to reach the height of the low ceiling. Each had its own small label with markings she could not quite make out from that distance, and they were filled with organized rows of packets and pouches. Some were paper, others looked to be a waxy material to keep their contents drier. Other cubbies held neat rows of glass bottles in varying sizes and colors; a white marble mortar and pestle lay neatly in the center of the desk beside other instruments and measuring implements Juliette could not have named had she been asked.

The physician gestured to a piece of furniture resembling a low cushioned chaise without any sides or backrest. It was draped in crisp, clean white linen sheets.

"Please, be seated," he spoke softly, reassuringly.

Thomas helped her to the table and lowered her to sit. Juliette sighed in relief after the exertion of trying to maneuver in her skirts and impractical shoes; her ankle throbbed with a fierce, burning pain. She'd fallen hard when the selfless physician wrenched her back from certain catastrophe in the street, but she couldn't fault his efforts even if it had ended in injury. She flinched when she tried to move her foot experimentally. She prayed it wasn't broken.

Don't be ridiculous, she silently scolded herself for feeling the least bit ungrateful that her life had been spared. *Anything is better than being trampled.*

Juliette returned her attention to their surroundings. A small street-level window behind her emitted some warm afternoon light from the street. The occasional shadow of passing legs crossed the cloudy glass. To her left was another doorway, its door slightly ajar. The room within was dim, but she could make out a desk and some stacks of books—his study, perhaps?

Several frames hung in an orderly row on the wall beside the door-frame. The elegant script announced their owner's completion of several degrees of study, accolades and awards. The name emblazoned below was that of Dr. Ian McCullom.

A bell of recognition sounded within Juliette's skull. *Of course!* How could she not have made the connection?

Dr. McCullom was the latest rage amongst the health-conscious—and often deluded—*ton*. Scottish-born and, reputedly, quite good-looking, he was lately the preferred physician to the upper-class London elite. He catered to wealthy clientele, but, if the stories were to be believed, his treatments and practices were not the smoke and mirrors or antiquated practices of her grandparents' era. Word was, he was extremely well-educated and had purportedly studied beneath some of the greatest minds both in Britain and abroad on the Continent.

Every woman wanted to be able to say she was in his (handsome) capable hands, and every household wanted to have his interesting mind in attendance. He'd amassed an unbelievable amount of renown and a sterling reputation over the past several years—particularly for a Scotsman in London. McCullom had made his name introducing medical advancements into his treatments and had become known for his quick mind and sometimes unorthodox treatment methods which proved to have some astounding results never before witnessed. There were even some rumors that he'd been involved in the care and recovery of Viscount Sommerfeld after his mysterious, debilitating leg injury.

McCullom turned back to face Juliette and she was forced to admit to herself that the rumors of his attractiveness were far from truth. She was used to physicians being elderly gentlemen; quiet and unintimidating. What the women of the *ton* had been tittering about more and more frequently at the parties she'd attended did *not* do this man justice.

He was dangerous.

Part of what had caused her such distraction earlier in the street had been the shocking contrast of his well-groomed appearance to the rugged edge in his glittering blue eyes, the unnatural breadth of his shoulders and the height of his build. Dr. McCullom appeared to be more suited to wielding a claymore than an instrument of medicine. He had a broad jaw sharp as an axeblade, a strong nose, and bold brows a shade darker than his overlong chestnut hair.

Juliette swallowed convulsively.

No wonder women clamored to be in his care.

"You're Dr. Ian McCullom," Juliette finally croaked. His strong features softened some when he smiled. It was remarkably pleasant.

"Aye. I supposed we've foregone all polite niceties, haven't we? That does happen when one's life is threatened."

Juliette could have kicked herself for the silly, breathless laugh that escaped her lips. She prayed it came out more charming than she thought it had.

If it wasn't he showed no sign of noticing when he said, "Then you'll forgive me for being so forward as to ask for your name, since we've no mutual acquaintance here to perform the introductions?" He cocked a brow when she didn't immediately reply. "Did you hit your head in the fall?"

Juliette shook her head vigorously before he could reach out to check her skull for cracks. She was taken aback by the size of those hands; they could probably palm her entire head with ease. How did he possibly manage any of the finesse one would expect from a physician expected to perform delicate procedures?

"Lady Juliette Crawford. My brother is the Earl of Hopesend."

With polished manners, Dr. McCullom inclined his head and took her hand to bow over it. "A pleasure." His barely perceptible burr made the words almost like a purr that tickled every inch of her spine.

"Now," he righted himself and turned to Thomas. "If you will excuse us, lad. I need to examine her ladyship's injury."

The poor young footman's eyes widened. "If it's all the same, I think I should stay." He straightened his spine in an admirable show of protectiveness.

"I do not treat my patients with an audience, and I don't particularly believe the lady would enjoy having a young man look on as I treat her." The doctor's words were calm and even, but there was an undertone that indicated he usually got his way; plainly, the statement brooked no discussion. Torn between a well-intentioned sense of duty and an innate desire for self-preservation, Thomas began to splutter until Juliette stepped in to rescue him.

"You may wait just outside the room, Thomas. It will be fine if the door remains open a crack if you would like to keep an eye on me." This seemed to assuage his indecision. He strengthened his narrow jaw and gave a nod before bowing out of the room. He shot the doctor what she supposed was meant to be a warning look, but it was rather less impressive when aimed at a man who was easily two stone his superior.

Dr. McCullom watched the footman leave and he made a point of closing the door several inches more than the lad had allowed. He turned back to her and Juliette became suddenly aware that she'd never been so alone with a man to whom she was unrelated. As if sensing her nerves, McCullom's face softened. His tone was gentler than when he'd spoken to Thomas; this was quite clearly the tone he used with overwrought and ailing ladies. With the faint lilt to his inflection, she found she didn't mind it as much as she might have had it come from anyone else.

"Now, my lady; if you would please remove your stocking so I might examine your injured ankle."

Juliette's thoughts came to a screeching halt.

"I beg your pardon?" Had he asked her what she thought he had?

"I assure you, I've no ill intentions," he reassured her; "I merely need to see the limb to assess the best course of treatment."

She met his eyes but saw no subterfuge. There was no spark of mischief or lechery. Still…to allow a man such a liberty…even a doctor. Juliette scolded herself. Were he not half so handsome, would she have been quite so nervous? What a silly notion. He was simply doing his job. And he was well-respected. Surely something would have been said by now were he mistreating his female clients.

Reading her indecision with his uncanny sensibilities, McCullom sought to reassure her once again. "It truly is the best way for me to determine if the limb requires a splint or a wrap. I can always perform the examination over your stocking, but I want to be sure the bruising is not extensive."

Convinced, Juliette nodded. McCullom excused himself to wash his hands and allow her some privacy. She waited several heartbeats before getting to her feet as best as she could. Not without a great deal of difficulty and whispered curses, she was able to pull aside her skirts, unbutton and kick off her shoe, undo the tapes holding up her thigh-high stocking, and slide off the undergarment.

She'd just regained her seat when there was a light rap at the door. She bid the knocker to enter and McCullom's large frame filled the doorway. It took her but a moment to realize that he'd doffed his coat and was only in his charcoal-colored waistcoat and shirtsleeves. If it was possible, he seemed even larger without the confining fabric of his well-cut coat.

Suddenly aware that she was still holding her silk stocking in her hand, Juliette hastily shoved it beneath her hip. If he noticed, then he was kind enough to say nothing. He closed the door and left a gap only an inch or two wide, as he'd promised he would. It afforded them some privacy but allowed Thomas to hear anything should she require his presence.

McCullom gave her a reassuring smile that did funny things to the pit of her stomach.

"There, now; let us see what damage has been done." He knelt before her and Juliette realized he was waiting for her to lift the hem of her skirts. As awkward as the encounter was, he was affording her every nicety possible and respecting her space as much as he could.

Her cheeks burned painfully when he began examining her foot and ankle with focused interest. When he asked permission to touch her, she just about expired on the spot. She had to avert her eyes and focus on one of the documents mounted on the wall. Though supremely gentle, the sight of her foot in his enormous hands made her realize that he really could snap her in two if he so wished. It was an unexpectedly heady realization.

Dr. McCullom proceeded to tenderly palpate the swollen joint with surprisingly gentle fingers, flexing it this way and that, stopping just shy of when he would cause her pain. Juliette watched the top of his head as he worked quietly and efficiently.

"I don't believe I truly thanked you for your quick reactions," Juliette murmured, fascinated by the tingling sensation of the pads of his large fingers on her foot and ankle.

What might it feel like to have those hands elsewhere…?

"There's no need to thank me," he replied, still focused on her foot. He moved aside her skirts to see just how high the ugly purple bruise and the corresponding swelling had traveled. The foreign sensation of his fingers against the back of her calf sent a pleasant chill down her spine.

So in tune with the human body, McCullom noticed the slight movement she made. His eyes flew to her face.

"My apologies; was that painful?"

Juliette quickly shook her head and he turned back to his examination.

*****

Ian was always detached and professional during his examinations. He'd seen many a disrobed woman and even been outright solicited for *other* services alongside the medical care he provided, but never before had he been so distracted by a patient. And by such an inane body part as a foot and ankle.

It was ridiculous, but it was the truth.

He silently chided himself, but a part of him couldn't help but appreciate the dainty toes and sweetly turned ankle—despite its obvious injury. An ugly blue-and-purple bruise marred the pale, perfect flesh. The swelling, while obvious, was not worse than to be expected. What he could see of her calf was lean and smooth to the touch…

Ian had to force himself away. He replaced her skirts and cleared his throat.

"Your ankle is badly sprained, but I do not believe there is a break," he said as he stood. "You will need to stay off the leg completely for at least the next week," he added, turning toward the nearby desk.

"But that is impossible!" Her posture slumped dejectedly.

Ian barely resisted rolling his eyes as every ounce of attraction he felt rapidly melted into a puddle at his feet. She might be attractive, but there was nothing so different about this woman from any other English lady he'd thus encountered. They were more concerned with their social calendar than anything else, to a one.

"Should you wish to not do permanent damage then I fear you'll have to postpone the rest of your shopping and forego any balls for the time being," he apologized somewhat insincerely. He didn't know why this struck him so hard, but he was more than a little bit disappointed that there was nothing to separate Lady Juliette from any other young chit of the *ton*—of course, not to say that anything would have happened had she truly been a unique specimen. She was the sister of an earl and he…Ian was an orphan son of an impoverished territory whose people were generally looked upon as savages. Just because he'd managed to claw his way from starvation and persecution to attain some knowledge and comfortability didn't mean he was necessarily much different from whence he'd come. Now he was simply more of a unique oddity; an object of interest.

"I don't care about any of that," her voice sliced through his musings and he met those captivating eyes of hers. "I have a meeting of my ladies' reading society and I've so been looking forward to discussing *Dushenka*."

Ian had been expecting her to protest, but practically any other response might have been more likely than that one. What lady lamented being kept from a literary circle—and one that discussed Eighteenth-century Russian poets, for that matter? He checked her face for sincerity and read only disappointment in her eyes and the slight downturn of her pretty rosebud lips.

Silently, he strode to the nearby worktable and carefully weighed and measured a packet of powders. He dispensed them into a waxed pouch and carefully folded it closed. He retrieved a rolled length of clean, white linen strips and held out the packet to Lady Juliette.

"Take this and mix a spoonful with your tea—the sugar will cut the bitterness. It will help with the pain. I can wrap the ankle to give it some stability, but allow it to rest when you are abed and remove the wrappings to allow it to breathe."

She nodded gratefully and accepted the packet from him, seeming to take great pains that their fingers didn't touch. He watched for a moment as she turned the packet over with her graceful hands before he knelt once more and did his best to ignore his traitorous heart as he pushed aside the hem of her skirts and began to wrap her ankle. She proved to be a keen student and paid close attention to his technique as he wove the linen around her ankle and foot in an orderly and strategic pattern.

"Should you require anything," Ian began as he retrieved one of his cards and handed it to her; "please send notice. I should like to call upon you in the next couple of days to see how you're healing."

"Oh, that truly isn't necessary," she tried to protest, but he allowed no discussion on the matter.

"It is the least I can do since I am partially responsible for your injury."

"Hardly!" she gave a breathy little laugh. "You were not the one who pushed me; you saved me from being squashed beneath the wheels of a cabbage cart."

"Still," Ian retorted, unable to hide his smile; "I never leave a patient's treatment in the hands of another. I always see my patients through." Her remarkable gaze met his and Ian found he momentarily forgot how to breathe.

"Very well, Dr. McCullom," she conceded. "I shall await your call." In response, she extracted a copy of her own engraved, extremely costly calling cards from her small beaded reticule which had, somewhat miraculously, managed to remain strapped to her wrist. Ian scanned the flourishing calligraphy and recognized the wealthy Mayfair address. He'd treated a neighboring dowager's gout just the other day.

Ian proceeded to delve into his extensive and necessary knowledge of the English peerage and quickly recalled how Lady Juliette's brother—her twin—was a powerful political Goliath and had made quite the waves in Parliament. Despite his relatively young age, his fiery vehemence and oratory prowess were legendary. He traveled in slightly different circles than those that involved Ian's work so he'd not met the Earl in person, though that would undoubtedly change when he came to call later in the week.

Ian beckoned to the footman standing vigil outside the office door. The lad poked his head into the room and Ian instructed him to retrieve the lady's carriage to convey her home for rest.

"But, sir…" he hesitated and looked between Ian and his employer's sister. "I don't think I should leave." Ian barely resisted the urge to huff an impatient sigh.

"Then how do you propose Lady Juliette get home? My housekeeper, Mrs. Brown, should be in the kitchen. You may ask her to serve as a chaperone if you so wish. Have the carriage brought 'round to the back alley entrance. We shouldn't like to have the lady gawked at even more than has already happened today." The young footman nodded and he was quickly replaced by Ian's plump, kind-eyed housekeeper. The older woman took the opportunity to seat herself in one of the chairs in the waiting room just outside of the door and continue her careful mending of one of Ian's shirts.

Ian proceeded to tidy his work area and do his best to ignore the caress he swore he felt as Lady Juliette's eyes watched his every movement. Her gaze was a palpable entity, hovering over his shoulder and pressing its length against his back in a warm, intimate fashion. A glass vial slipped through his fingers and clinked to the wooden table-top; the sound seemed to echo in the silent room.

"Oh!" Lady Juliette suddenly chimed in as if the thought had just occurred to her, or she could no longer bear the silence—Ian suspect-ed it was the latter. "May I offer you payment for your services?" she offered and he heard her rustling around for her reticule. Ian turned and waved away her offer of payment.

"Please, no."

"Are you certain? I feel as if I have put you out so." There was an uncertain gleam in her eyes.

"Truly." Ian smiled reassuringly.

A moment of companionable silence passed between them. Was Ian imagining things, or was there a tiny flame of attraction blossom-ing in the space separating their bodies? He knew he felt it in the way his fingers ached to touch the softness of her skin and determine if her lips tasted as sweet as they appeared; but did she feel it as well?

It might seem so because she could no longer hold his gaze and there was a telling, delicate pink tint rising on the crests of her cheeks.

Before he could stop her, Lady Juliette made a move to stand. She had either forgotten the weakness in her ankle, or she was desperate to take leave of his office because she moved far too quickly. Ian rushed to steady her before she fell.

"You really shouldn't stand," he gently admonished. Her hands clutched his forearms as a grimace flitted across her face.

"Thomas will be returning shortly with the carriage; I promise I shall stay off of my feet when I am home."

Ian's eyes ran the length of her body and hesitated at a swath of ivory fabric standing in stark contrast to her skirts. A small bell from the door indicated the footman's arrival. Ian smoothly snagged the fabric and balled it up in his fist before the footman entered.

"The carriage has been brought 'round, My Lady," said the lad, eyeing their closeness.

"Thank you, Thomas." Did Ian imagine the slight tremor in her voice?

"May I assist you—"

"That won't be necessary," Ian cut off the footman a moment before he swept Lady Juliette into his arms and lifted her against his chest. Her little breathless gasp of surprise teased something deep inside his soul. She wrapped her arms around his neck to steady herself and he was instantly overcome with a warm, sweet scent. It was much more delicate than anything else that was so *en vogue* these days... and far more alluring.

Ian indicated that the footman should lead the way; the lad hesitated only a moment before he rushed to open the doors for them. He was obviously more than a little shocked at Ian's actions but was unsure of what to say or how to handle the situation. He settled for accepting it when his mistress did not protest.

Ian held Lady Juliette close to his chest, taking pleasure in her slight weight in his arms, as he exited his townhouse and found a black-lacquered, well-sprung carriage pulled by a team of perfectly matched horses as blue as midnight. The conveyance spoke of the undeniable wealth and power of their owner. When he'd been a boy, Ian had never thought to see such a vehicle, let alone be climbing into one to deposit an injured young woman upon the plush velvet squab.

He stepped aloft and ducked into the carriage, the springs creaking with his added weight, and he settled Lady Juliette on the overstuffed forward-facing seat. Her arms slid from his neck, though he still felt their warmth seared into the skin beneath his clothing.

"I wish you the best, Lady Juliette," Ian murmured and then took her hand in his. He pressed what he held into her palms.

Her face burned and her eyes flew to his when she realized what he'd done.

"I didn't think you'd want your footman to see your stocking stuck to your skirts," he spoke in a low tone and gave her a wink. "I will call upon you in a few days to check on your progress," he added normally.

"Thank you," she said in a small voice as Ian ducked back out of the carriage. He stepped back down to the cobblestones and watched as Thomas latched the door before jumping onto the back of the carriage as they lurched into motion.

Ian watched them trundle down the wide alleyway and pondered what, exactly, had made him offer to call upon Lady Juliette in her home. He hadn't lied when he'd said he personally monitored each of his patients, but he knew very well his schedule was already tightly packed. An astonishing number of peers were on a waiting list to be seen by him—something else his younger self would never have believed possible. He made a very good living by being in such high demand, but it left little time for other pursuits.

Still…something drew him to this Russian poetry-reading woman who was unlucky enough to nearly tumble headfirst into the wheels of a cart.

Chapter Two

Two days later, Ian found himself standing alone in the echoing entryway of a stunning, richly appointed Townhome in Mayfair. The newly-renovated residence took up nearly an entire block on its own and was one of the largest and most opulent on the street with its soaring columns and immaculate white-washed façade. There would once have been a time when Ian would have been intimidated by such wealth, but if his time as a physician to the elite had taught him anything, it was that even those with money were mortal and, quite often, they suffered from more weaknesses than those of a lower class—they simply possessed the money and the training to hide it better.

The earl's butler had accepted his calling card and disappeared several minutes prior. Ian hadn't immediately been turned away, so at least Lady Juliette was receiving callers.

As he was examining the ceiling painted to resemble a wispy summer sky, the stony-faced butler returned, took Ian's hat and cloak, and led him down a hallway to an overtly masculine study. There, behind a desk set against a backdrop of soaring bookcases filled with a veritable rainbow of leather-bound tomes, sat a man. He was younger than Ian, but the intense flash in his icy blue eyes spoke of a keen intelligence and knowledge of his own power which spoke of a much more mature, self-assured age. The desk before him was piled high with correspondence and blank parchment, each organized in its orderly stack. His raven hair was perfectly groomed and his dark jacket and bright blue waistcoat were immaculate. Everything from the powerful tilt to his chin to the confident set of his shoulders spoke of impeccable breeding and the knowledge of his place in this world— something Ian would never possess, no matter how highly-regarded he was, how much wealth he managed to amass, or how he dressed.

Even all these years later, Ian remained keenly aware of the fact that he'd be nothing more than a Scotsman: unlanded, untitled, and viewed as lesser because of his coloring, his speech, and his birthplace. These people would clamor to have him use his knowledge to cure their ailments and they would brag about how they'd been the recipients of his knowledge and talents, but he'd never be more than an elevated servant to them. He was forever caught in an awkward position where he was not their equal, but he was more than hired help; he was often invited to attend parties as thank-yous or bribes to be moved up on his waiting list, but he was forever sullied by the sin of working for a living.

The earl behind the desk was one of those men who was so far above Ian's station that Ian was an ant in his view. He scurried about his daily life and was not even a minor distraction in his world. They were from different worlds.

When he noticed Ian being shown into the room, the young man stood in greeting. A glance around the room told Ian that his patient, Lady Juliette, was nowhere to be found.

"Dr. McCullom," the Earl of Hopesend greeted Ian with a pleasant enough smile. The tilt of his lips was strikingly similar to his sister's, as was the shape of his eyes, but the appearance was far less kind on him. "It appears I have you to thank for my sister's wellbeing. I appreciate your quick action and treatment of her."

Ian inclined his head and responded politely. "I was merely doing my duty, My Lord."

"Your reputation quite precedes you. I admit that I made some inquiries after Juliette returned and described your encounter." The earl gestured to a nearby calf-leather chair, offering Ian a seat. "My sister is quite dear to me. I am eternally grateful to you for all you have done." While the words were sincere, there was a cool formality to his tone.

"Thank you, no," Ian declined the earl's invitation to sit. "I have a rather busy schedule today and I must make my visit brief."

"I understand," he nodded, reaching for a nearby drawer and removing a book of banknotes. "I would like to reward you for your services. What do you feel is a fair sum? Our family physician, Dr. Blythe, shall take over her care from here."

"While I appreciate your offer, My Lord, I must decline payment. And I would much rather see Lady Juliette's care through, myself. I never leave a patient in the hands of another physician if it can be helped." Ian watched as the younger man's middle finger tapped against the book of banknotes, either through frustration or thoughtfulness, he wasn't at first certain. His next words, however, provided Ian with his answer.

"I assure you," the earl pushed back; "Dr. Blythe is more than capable of handling this situation. It is, after all, merely a turned ankle."

"With all due respect, your physician is not me."

An arched brow told Ian exactly what the earl thought of the comment. To many, Ian's words might seem more than a little conceited, but if they'd been in Ian's shoes these last several years as he cleaned up the messes left scattered about by patients clutching onto superstitious cures and physicians unwilling to reassess antiquated practices, then they might feel the same. He'd witnessed firsthand just how wrong simple treatments could go.

The men stared one another down for several tense minutes before the earl, rather surprisingly, capitulated rather than throw Ian out on his ear.

"Very well," he groused. "My sister is upstairs in her sitting room. You have permission for no more than ten minutes of her time; that should be more than sufficient." It wasn't a question. "Francis will show you the way." A raised finger signaled the silent manifestation of the butler at Ian's side. "He will see you out when you are finished."

The banknotes were dropped back into the desk drawer before the earl's attention was quickly shifted to another stack of papers atop his desk. Ian was summarily dismissed and, biting his tongue, he sketched a quick bow and followed the butler from the study.

Together, they traversed the hallway and climbed the thickly carpeted stairs to the third floor. Everything Ian saw spoke of many generations of wealth and privilege. Paintings several centuries old graced alcoves and gold-gilded fixtures were scattered throughout. This was certainly not a household that burned anything less than the finest beeswax candles; there was not so much as a hint of the acrid smoke of cheap fuel. The plush carpet runner made their movements all but entirely silent. Its rich navy and burgundy hues swirled beneath their every step, underscoring the frivolity of the class.

Ian was pondering as much when he was shown to a private sitting room. The walls were papered in delicately patterned rose-pink and ivory. Lacey curtains framed tall windows on the far wall, against which sat a delicate cherry wood writing desk.

"Dr. McCullom!"

Ian's attention snapped to his patient where she sat in a cloud of gauzy daffodil-colored skirts, her injured leg elevated upon a pillow embroidered with greenery and rosebuds. Ian had all but convinced himself that his memories of her beauty were exaggerated, born of uncharacteristically fanciful musings, but that had been the boldest of lies. Lady Juliette with her midnight hair and unnaturally captivating eyes was stunning, indeed.

And when she smiled at him, his lungs froze in his chest.

"I wasn't expecting you to call today." She smiled in a warm greeting which revealed dimples in both of her smooth cheeks, and set aside her book. Despite her injury, she still appeared as composed and elegant as a queen upon her throne.

"I did say I would call upon you to review your progress."

"So you did." Her smile and the flash of her pearl-white teeth actually made his knees weaken. "Please! Do sit down." She gestured to the nearby chair. "Allow me to send for some refreshments."

"I fear I must make this visit brief," Ian declined, though it was the last thing he wanted to do. "His Lordship made it quite clear I had only ten minutes of your time with which to perform my examination and be on my way." He spared a glance at the porcelain-framed clock upon the mantle. "And I have only six of those minutes remaining."

She emitted a breathy laugh through her nose in response. It was far from proper, but Ian found it immensely charming. "Ethan loses track of time when he works. He'll hardly notice if you overstay by a few minutes." Ian sincerely doubted that the earl would be so flippant about having another man in his house and dancing attention upon his sister, but he decided to take Lady Juliette's word for it. He strode over to the chair to which she'd gestured and set his bag by his feet. She then requested the disapproving butler tug upon the bellpull. An intricate dance was performed in which the request for refreshments was conveyed and a suitable chaperone in the form of the housekeeper—a woman of slightly beyond middling age with a granite face and steel-gray hair beneath her cap—sat in the corner like a watchful gargoyle.

It wasn't long before two maids returned with a full service of tea, shortbread, and small roast beef sandwiches carved into dainty triangles. It would forever escape Ian how efficient and well-prepared these households were. Could they have possibly begun their preparations as soon as he'd set foot in the door? How else could the tray have been ready with such expediency?

"Allow me," he said when Lady Juliette leaned forward to pour for them both. A man who had been born to nothing and lived a simple life, it always made him supremely uncomfortable to be served by others. It was bad enough that the maids had scrambled to serve this repast, he couldn't very well defer to societal norms and allow Lady Juliette to inconvenience herself and prepare their tea. His conscience wouldn't allow it.

She seemed taken aback by the gesture but gladly accepted the cup and saucer after he'd added a splash of milk and a single cube of sugar per her instructions.

As he sat back in the impossibly dainty chair, he noticed that the book she'd been reading was, indeed, in Russian.

"*Vam nravitsya vasha kniga?*" he asked, tilting his chin toward the book on the arm of the sofa; *Are you enjoying your book?* She'd moved on from Bogdanovich and was—rather impressively—tackling Karamzin's *The Pantheon*.

Lady Juliette's remarkable eyes widened and her lush mouth split into a devastatingly beautiful grin. "*Da! Mne ochen' nravitsya!*" *Yes! I am very much!* "I have read many of the originals the author compiled and translated into his native tongue, so it has been interesting to compare the texts." Her eyes glowed with delight. "It's all rather elegant and flowing. *Ty govorish' po-russki?*" She asked if he spoke Russian.

Ian winced and replied in English. "Passably."

"More than passably," Lady Juliette gushed, inordinately pleased to have found someone else who spoke the language.

"Not nearly as well as you, my lady. You must be fluent if you are reading a novel."

The blush on her cheeks was more than becoming, it was beguiling. "Languages are a bit of a hobby of mine," she admitted. "I've always had an ear for them; my parents and my brother have helped me cultivate it with tutors. I find I enjoy reading literature written as the authors intended. This one presents a particularly interesting linguistic comparison."

A smile toyed with the corner of Ian's mouth. "*Quelles autres langues connaissez-vous? Français?*" *What other languages do you know? French?* he asked, the lilting sounds rolling off his tongue.

"*Mais bien sûr!*" she replied brightly; *But of course!*

"*Y habla español también?*" Ian asked if she spoke Spanish as well.

"*Naturalmente!*" she answered with a grin.

"*Sicuramente non parli anche italiano?*" Having spent so much time in Italy, this last was one language with which he was quite familiar and confident in his pronunciation.

"*Non mi ingannerai, dottor McCullom. La famiglia di mia madre è italiana.*" Her bubble of laughter was like the ringing of the most sonorous of bells. *You will not trick me, Dr. McCullom. My mother's family is from Italy.* This explained her dark coloring.

Ian's eyes narrowed playfully, deciding to extend even more of a test—one close to his heart. She had responded perfectly thus far, but he wanted to see how she'd react to the next one. "*Is e boireannach sgoinneil a th'annad, ach tha mi teagmhach gu bheil cànan mo dhaoine anns an leabharlann agad.*"

Her lips parted, but she had no answer for him. "Say it again," she asked, more out of eagerness to hear the words than it was a command. His heart skipped a beat and he complied.

"That was lovely," she breathed. "What language was that?"

"Scots Gaelic," he replied, his eyes flashing over to the housekeeper-turned-gargoyle in the corner. It wasn't all that long ago that the language was outlawed, along with so many other parts of his heritage. It was the tongue of his childhood, the native language of his mother. He'd been raised in the Highlands before fortune smiled upon him and he had attended school in Edinburgh.

"And what does it mean?" she asked, drawing his attention back to her rapt expression.

"'You are a brilliant woman, but I doubt the language of my people is in your library.'" It was difficult to keep the grin off his face, especially when she laughed again.

"I like your humor, Dr. McCullom," she rested her cheek on her hand and gazed across at him. Ian felt his heart trip once more. It had been decades since he'd blushed like a green lad, but he felt his cheeks heat dangerously in response.

He didn't know what came over him, but he leaned forward and spoke low and slow, *"Tha mi a' guidhe gun stadadh an saoghal a' tionndadh agus mar sin cha tàinig am mionaid seo gu crìch."*

I wish the world would stop turning so this moment never ended.

Her dark, elegantly arched brows twitched in bafflement as her mind turned the unfamiliar sounds over and over again.

"What did you say this time?"

Ian finished his cup of tea rather than translate for her. "You said you enjoyed languages, Lady Juliette; I have just given you a new challenge with which to occupy yourself while you recuperate. Now," he added as he set the cup on the table between them and stood; "I wouldn't want to overstay my welcome. With your permission, may I examine your injury?"

"Of course." Lady Juliette shifted her skirts to give him access to her ankle. She was an excellent pupil and had done an admirable job of wrapping the joint. She'd rather scandalously foregone a stocking on that leg, but it made Ian's examination far simpler. He noted the angry purple and yellow bruising and tender swelling, but they hadn't spread. She did flinch as he palpated and tested the flexion, but she didn't cry out.

"Are you taking the medicine I provided?" he asked, trying to ignore how soft and pale her skin was.

"Yes, but I've run low."

"Then it's a good thing I've brought more with me."

"How well-prepared you are, Doctor."

Ian gave her a small smile as he re-wrapped her injury. "You still have tenderness, but that is to be expected. I still do not suspect a break, but you will need to continue your rest." He rifled through his leather bag and set another packet of pain powder on the table. "This has enough doses to see you through the week, but do not hesitate to send word should you require more. Many apothecaries can supply it, but I created this mixture myself and can vouch for its purity and the dosage."

"Then I will certainly contact you should I require more. Thank you." She averted her eyes as if thinking about her next words and then deciding to say them anyway. "I do hope Ethan wasn't too rude to you and made you feel as if you needed to rush off."

"Of course not," Ian fibbed lightly. She didn't need to know just how much her brother hadn't wanted Ian to see her; besides, he could hold his own. It took a great deal more than a few glares and gruff words to intimidate him.

"He's always been more than a little overprotective," she added by way of explanation. Ian supposed he would be too if he had a treasure such as Lady Juliette to protect.

"Understandable for any brother," Ian reassured her and bowed deeply. "It has been a pleasure, Lady Juliette. Continue your rest for this week and next. Begin your physical activity slowly and do not overdo it."

"Yes, Doctor," she replied cheekily. Ian had to look away from her smile. "Thank you again; for everything."

"Think nothing of it," he murmured and turned on his heel, knowing full well he'd likely never see this bewitching woman again. Ian recognized it was for the best; this attraction he felt could never be realized and would surely only bring trouble.

Chapter Three

"I'd no idea they made such attractive physicians!" tittered Fanny, Juliette's incorrigible maid. In any other household, the girl would likely have been sacked long ago for her overly familiar manner of speaking, but Juliette had always found her amusing and the maid was a genius with a pair of hot tongues so she'd kept her around with strict instructions to stay out of Ethan's way, lest he catch wind of Juliette's leniency.

"Hush, Fanny," Juliette murmured, schooling her features to remain stern...no matter that she completely agreed with the maid's assessment.

Half of her had expected Dr. McCullom to not follow through on his promise to take time from his schedule to call upon her and review her progress; he was, after all, a very busy man. When his arrival had been announced—and he'd somehow made it past her gatekeeper of a brother!—she'd felt more than a tiny thrill at the imminent prospect of seeing him again.

Were his eyes really that captivating, or had her fanciful imagination taken over her memories?

Juliette hadn't been disappointed, to say the least.

Then, when he'd spoken to her in all those languages…

As soon as he'd quit the room, she'd hurriedly scribbled down the phonetic spelling of the phrase he'd spoken in Gaelic. Once a child whose fragile health prevented her from playing with other children and now a sheltered woman all but hidden away from most of the world, she always adored a linguistic challenge. It had been hours since the doctor's departure and she was still skimming the note, trying to figure out how she could decipher the message. Who could possibly speak the language fluently enough to help her translate it?

There was a single curt knock upon her bedchamber door before her brother entered. Ethan was already dressed for dinner, though it was to be only the two of them that evening. It felt like it had been just them forever, especially since their parents' deaths sixteen years prior. Ethan had taken on the role of an adult far earlier than he should have and, with his natural inclination to studiousness and severity, he'd taken it on with all the gravity of a man at least twice his age.

They shared the same light eyes of their father and thick, dark hair of their mother's Italian heritage. Juliette's features were a softer version of her twin's patrician looks with a strong nose and expressive dark brows. He stood tall and straight as an oak, refusing to bend to the elements and sure in his firmly-rooted place in the world, and he took frequent rides through Hyde Park for air and exercise. There was no doubt her brother was an intimidating man—and not just because of his lofty title. Juliette knew, however, that Ethan had a very deep soft spot for her. He may be overprotective and often frustrating in his manner and rules, but she never forgot that it came from a place of love. They were all they had left in the world.

"I thought I'd see what Dr. McCullom said after his examination," he said, clasping his hands behind his ramrod-straight back. Juliette tucked the Gaelic note into the book in her lap and closed it.

"Frankly, I am surprised that you weren't informed." *Or that you hadn't already asked the housekeeper.* As her brother and male guardian, Ethan should have been informed of her well-being. She barely suppressed a smile, knowing in her heart that Dr. McCullom had avoided doing so on purpose.

"The doctor informed Francis that he had another call to make presently and 'did not have the time to speak with me again.'" It was obvious that Ethan was more than mildly irked by this; he was not a man used to being brushed off. "Can you believe that?" he huffed. "He, a physician, believes his time is more valuable than mine."

Juliette rolled her eyes at his haughty dramatics. "I am sure Dr. McCullom did, indeed, have another appointment he needed to keep. You and I both know his reputation." She continued to speak, not giving Ethan a chance to continue grousing. "I am still under instructions to rest." She nibbled her lower lip, knowing this was a perfect lead-in to the problem she needed to remedy. "I fear I will be unable to travel for my reading society meeting this week," she sighed pathetically. She had to let Ethan believe her plan was *his* idea. "And I was *so* looking forward to it."

"Well that is quite the shame," Ethan murmured, having turned his attention to a small porcelain bird upon her dressing table. The finch was taking flight from a twisted branch dripping with delicate flowers. It had been their mother's. The piece looked so fragile in her brother's large hand.

"I've finished reading the piece and everything, but now I shall have no one to discuss it with," she sighed.

Ethan frowned and gently set down the statue. "What did you read?"

"Poetry," she offered, she hoped not too quickly, secretly crossing her fingers and hoping he didn't ask whose poetry. She wanted to maintain his disillusionment that they only read sweet, fluffy literature suitable for the fragile female mind for as long as possible. Ethan tapped his thumb on his hip.

"Why don't you invite your reading society here for the meeting? Surely the Duchess of Morton won't object to moving the meeting just this once given the circumstances. The two of you have grown quite close, have you not?"

Juliette clapped her hands and held them to her chest. "Oh, Ethan! What a brilliant idea!" she gushed. "I wish I had thought of that." *She had...*

Pleased that he'd come up with a solution to her predicament and could come to her rescue, her brother's face split into one of his rare smiles. "How much trouble can a women's reading society get into?" *Quite a bit...* "Besides, I've plans for Thursday so you needn't worry about inconveniencing me." *She hadn't...* But she'd had a feeling Ethan was going to be out anyway.

He usually was.

She, on the other hand, counted the hours between her infrequent outings. In fact, the incident precipitating her turned ankle had been a rare occasion during which Ethan had let her out of his sight in public. At the age of six-and-twenty, she was very firmly upon the shelf and should have generally been afforded more freedoms as a spinster, but those rules simply didn't sit well with Ethan. If anything, he'd become more protective of her over the years and felt it was absurd that a woman should be less monitored as she aged—there were, after all, the same dangers and evils in the world for a girl of sixteen as a woman of twenty-six.

Luckily for Juliette, her brother still believed her insistence that the reading society founded and coordinated by the Duchess of Morton was a simple ladies' gathering. He knew nothing of their incendiary discussions or how they very often read books usually deemed "unsuitable" or "not intended for gentlewomen of their sensibilities or breeding." She loved the reading society and the freedom it afforded her, almost as much as she adored the woman who ran it. Lady Morton's absentee husband allowed her to run practically roughshod over London. The young duchess had founded the club as a way in which to occupy herself with some close friends and carve out her niche in society. A longtime friend of the duchess's, Juliette had been one of the group's original members.

For years, they'd gathered together once each week to talk about inappropriate literature, eat, and revel in unchaperoned behavior. Gradually, more like-minded women were invited and their numbers had grown over the years to admit friends and other women who longed for an escape. For sheltered women like Juliette, this reading society was her brief respite from her mundane life. She loved her twin, but she missed the days so long ago now when he'd just been her brother and not responsible for her in every sense. The burden and his title had made him far too serious.

Satisfied with his decision, Ethan quit the room with the promise to come back in twenty minutes to collect her for supper and assist her down the stairs. Excited by the opportunity to host her friends and their reading society, Juliette snatched up a nearby sheaf of paper and jotted off a note to the Duchess of Morton briefly explaining her injury. She kept the details vague because she knew she'd have to retell it all over again to the group anyway. Juliette didn't worry that Lady

Morton would have an objection to the change in venue; she'd much rather their group get together than have an integral member missing due to injury. She hobbled over to the bellpull and rang for Fanny. There were still a few minutes with which she could begin the preparations before Ethan returned to escort her to supper.

A few days later, her plan firmly in place, Juliette sat comfortably in the front sitting room with her foot propped up on a pillow. Ethan, rather predictably, watched the clock on the mantle until he could dash off without being intercepted by any of her guests. He dropped a quick brotherly kiss atop her head and left as hastily as possible.

Not long after that, Lady Morton was the first to arrive and was quickly followed by a steady stream of the other ladies. They were a motley crew of wives, spinsters, awkward debutantes, and other women who needed a place to belong. Juliette had come to feel this group was her second family. Likewise, they all displayed sincere concern over her injury. It was already three-quarters of an hour into the meeting and not a single book had been opened; the women were far too interested in Juliette's harrowing tale.

She recounted nearly being crushed beneath the wheels of an oncoming cart, and then being rescued by a strong, handsome Scotsman.

"Did he sweep you off your feet?" asked one of the women, her eyes owlish in awe behind her spectacles.

"What happened next?" demanded another, so invested that she sat so dangerously close to the edge of her chair Juliette feared she might tumble to the ground in a pouf of skirts.

"Ladies," chuckled Lady Morton, raising her hands in a placating gesture. "Lady Juliette cannot very well continue with her story if you keep talking over her. Now," her golden blond head whipped over to Juliette; "what did he look like?" The devilish tilt to the duchess's lips was almost intimidating in its intensity. Deciding Lady Morton's inquiry to be the most pressing, Juliette launched into a description of Dr. McCullom.

"For comparison, I would say he's of a similar height to my brother, though his build is rather more…rugged." Her word choice caused a titter amongst the women. That had been an apt description of Dr. McCullom with his broad, imposing build and his large hands. She remembered what it felt like to have his fingers assess her injury, to be swept into his arms as he carried her to the carriage. "His hair was a blend of brown and auburn," she continued. "And his eyes were dark blue." She pictured his strong features, deep-set eyes and angular jaw. She'd never felt such a thrill just thinking about a man…to be fair, though, she hadn't been allowed to be around all that many men with which to have tested this out.

"He sounds positively dangerous!" one of the women squealed.

"Oh no, not at all!" Juliette shook her head. "In fact, it turned out that he was a physician. He so kindly treated my ankle after rescuing me."

"A Scottish physician?" inquired the fiery-haired lady seated beside Lady Morton on the sofa. Of course, this would interest Lady Sommerfeld; she was of Scottish heritage on her mother's side and had more than a passing interest in medicine. Juliette nodded enthusiastically.

"He wound up being the Dr. Ian McCullom! The very one!"

Lady Sommerfeld's eyes lit up and her lips curled into a blindingly beautiful smile. "I believe your story, Lady Juliette, and I'm finding the image of Ian as a knight in shining armor to be quite fascinating. I think it suits his personality quite well."

Ian? Suits his personality?

Did the viscountess know Dr. McCullom personally? Intimately?

Juliette's stomach plummeted to the floor. As if sensing the shift, Lady Sommerfeld clarified. "I've known him for years! He studied medicine beneath my uncle when I lived in Edinburough." The explanation only made Juliette feel momentarily better before mortification took over. Here she'd been gossiping and speaking of a man and entirely ignorant of the fact that one of his longtime friends was sitting only feet away. Juliette's cheeks flared; she suddenly wished for a miraculous recovery of her ankle because she wanted nothing more than to dash from the room and bury her head in her bed.

"He is also our personal physician," added Mrs. Odette Stratford, Lady Sommerfeld's sister-in-law. She was one of the newer members of their fold, though she'd likely be retiring for confinement soon. She was a petite, curvaceous woman and there was no hiding her ripe, rounded stomach any longer.

"Ian is the only one we trust with the care of our families," Lady Sommerfeld supplied.

They were always so sweet, these ladies, so they did their best to ease Juliette's embarrassment.

"Objectively, I must agree he is quite dashing," Mrs. Stratford smiled. "Though no one better say a word to my husband." She shot a warning glance to the rest of the women. "I don't blame you one bit for finding him attractive."

Suddenly, Lady Sommerfeld's brows rose and her lips formed into a grin all of them had long since learned boded for something mischievous. "You know, Lady Juliette…Ian is coming to dinner next Friday…perhaps you and the earl should attend as well." Juliette's cheeks burned furiously when she realized this was an attempt to throw her back together with Dr. McCullom. Before her mind could form a response, however, Lady Morton jumped on board.

"At the risk of being unbelievably rude, would you be willing to add another place setting?" the duchess gave an exaggerated bat of her eyes. "Surely you need one more woman to complete your number for dinner? I simply *have* to meet this man—this brilliant physician who is apparently also incredibly handsome."

"You're already married," interjected another woman good-naturedly; "leave the eligible men for the unattached women!" This earned a collective giggle, even from Juliette. Lady Morton smiled easily and flicked the comment away.

"Pish. My husband hasn't been in England in years anyway." She spoke flippantly, but all of them knew Lady Morton would never be unfaithful to her husband, no matter that he hadn't shown his face since the wedding ceremony...no matter that the tabloids were rife with the duke's scandalous behavior.

"Well, Lady Juliette?" Lady Sommerfeld reiterated her invitation. "Shall we count you and the earl amongst our numbers?"

"I don't know..." Juliette worried her lip. "Ethan and Dr. McCullom didn't exactly hit it off well at their first meeting." There was a shared glance between Lady Sommerfeld and Mrs. Stratford.

"*That* we can believe," said the red-haired woman. They shared a chuckle. "Despite having been his physician for several years now, Ian and my husband still butt heads like rams attempting to assert their dominance."
"Really?" Juliette's eyes widened.

Mrs. Stratford snickered and sat back in her chair. "Lord Sommerfeld still hasn't gotten over the fact that Dr. McCullom was in love with Meredith."

Juliette gasped and Lady Sommerfeld's head snapped to her sister-in-law.

"Wherever did you hear that?" she demanded.

"Why, Lily of course," Mrs. Stratford explained with a Gallic shrug. Lily was the third Stratford sibling and the only female. She had married Baron Shefford and they and their family spent most of the year on their estate in Kent.

Lady Sommerfeld rolled her indigo eyes. "I assure you, Ian is simply a dear friend and behaves in only the most proper of manners. Do think about the invitation, Lady Juliette; if nothing more than as a way to get out of this house after being cooped up with your injury."

"Thank you. I will certainly think on it." Who knew? Maybe Dr. McCullom would be pleased to see her again…he'd already gone out of his way to see her once. And maybe she could present him with a completed translation of the Gaelic phrase he'd left with her; surely he'd find that impressive.

Chapter Four

Ian was poring over his notes in his office late one evening. Fatigue clouded his sight and he rubbed his eyes with the heels of his hands. Knowing he wouldn't like what he saw, he still risked a glance at his timepiece. As suspected, it was even later than he'd estimated. This often happened when he was absorbed in his work; the night would come and go without his even realizing it.

The writing on the pages before him blurred before his eyes and forcing himself to stay awake wasn't doing any good. He'd reached the point where his mind was sluggish, which accomplished nothing of any value.

He doused all but one candle, carrying it with him as he moved through the building's lower floor. He checked the medicine cabinets where he locked away the more potent, hard-to-come-by medicines and herbs, and he ensured (twice) all the windows and doors were locked tight on both the lower and main floors before ascending the stairs to his private rooms above his business.

The building was three stories in height with a small, fully functional kitchen in the cellar alongside his medical practice. Although his current income allowed for it, he'd been supremely uncomfortable hiring a valet, butler, or bevy of maids. Instead, he made do with a single woman who would clean his private rooms while he was out during the day and then tidy his offices when he closed—except on these evenings when the distraction of his research kept him later than was reasonable. In addition to the cleaning, she also cooked him the simple foods he preferred, and, in return, he made it clear Mrs. Brown was welcome to bring along her young daughter on days when no one was available to care for her. He knew firsthand how difficult the world could be for a widowed mother of a young child. As daunting as the work seemed for an individual woman, it was a relatively easy job as far as cooking, cleaning, and housekeeping in London went. Growing up as he had, Ian was used to cleaning up after himself; he'd never had the luxuries a majority of his clients did. Most of his home's private rooms were devoid of furniture by choice and had been closed up. As a bachelor physician, what use did he have for a dining room when he ate alone? Or a parlor when he was always the one making the house calls? He didn't even think the extra bedrooms had been opened since he'd viewed the property before purchasing it; he couldn't even recall the color of the papering on the walls.

Ian's work was his life and his books were his friends.

Well…that was not entirely the truth. He did have some friends.

In addition to those connections he'd made in his travels, he'd become quite close with the new family of his longtime friend, Meredith. Though it had pained him to let her go when he realized she'd lost her heart to Viscount Sommerfeld, Ian took solace that Sommerfeld continued to treat Meredith well and made her undeniably happy. And if he didn't…well, then Ian knew a thousand ways to kill a man… quite a few of which were untraceable unless one knew what to look for.

Ian's foot froze above the first step when he heard the ring of a bell. He held his breath until it sounded again, then released it in one great whoosh. He rubbed his weary eyes with his thumb and forefinger. There was never to be a respite for him, was there? He couldn't in good conscience ignore the caller. Surely someone at this hour had a good reason to seek out a physician's care and, if they didn't, then he'd send them on their way with instructions to return at a more reasonable time the following morning.

Ian descended the stairs to the kitchen and entryway to his medical practice. He unlatched the porthole in the door—specifically designed for this situation when it could be dangerous to unlatch the door to just anyone in the dead of night—and found a familiar face looking back at him, her fiery curls mostly covered by a traveling cloak.

"Meredith?" Ian cursed and quickly slid aside the deadbolt and unlocked the door for her. There must be something wrong to have brought her to his offices unannounced and, from the looks of the dark carriage accompanied only by a single groom and driver, relatively unaccompanied. The viscount was nowhere in sight.

"Is everything alright, lass?" he ushered her inside, forgetting all propriety in his worry. His heart throbbed in concern; a part of him would likely always feel this way about her; it was impossible to stop his habit of caring after so many years, even when she had someone else to care for her now.

"I think so—I hope so," she stammered uncharacteristically and pushed back her hood. "I had to wait until George fell asleep before I could leave the house."

"He doesn't know where you are?" Ian frowned, knowing full well how upset *he* would be if he awoke to find his wife missing…and then discovered she'd slipped out to meet another man. "It's extremely late; you shouldn't have risked yourself coming here. You know these streets aren't always safe. And what would Sommerfeld do if he found out you'd snuck out to see me, of all people?" Ian raked a hand through his hair and then took note of Meredith's pallor, the slight tremble to her elegant hands. Setting aside his candle, he took her hands in his own and guided her over to a nearby wooden chair. "Take a deep breath. There; and now another. What is wrong? What is so urgent you had to come here without sending word first? You know I would have come to see you at the first opportunity."

Meredith nodded shakily. "It couldn't wait until morning; I couldn't wait any longer. I couldn't tell George without seeking out confirmation first." She then averted those glorious eyes of hers and shifted uncomfortably.

Ian squeezed her hands, his stomach sinking in dread. "Please, tell me, lass."

"I—I know how awkward this might be for you…and I will gladly seek out another physician if you decline. Besides, I believe I know the answer." She met his eyes. "I'm desperate for confirmation that I've conceived."

Everything froze for Ian; time, the air in his lungs, the blood in his veins.

As her physician, he'd known of her struggles over the last four years; the false alarms, the waning hope. And now…

He had no more designs upon her (he'd never pursue a married woman and especially not one so obviously invested in her love match), but this felt so much more solidifying and permanent. The tentatively hopeful glint in her eyes heralded the closing of a door upon a part of his life. He'd believed himself in love with this woman before him while she'd never seen him as more than a friend. An older brother. And now, if her suspicions were correct, she'd finally be starting a family of her own—something he knew she'd always craved with deep-seated desperation.

Though it pained him deep in his gut, Ian agreed with a nod of his head to examine her and provide his best assessment.

He showed her into his office and, as he scrubbed his hands, he inquired as to her symptoms. Was she ill in the morning? When was the date of her last courses? The last presented complications because her body had always been erratic. He then performed his examination, allowing her as much dignity and modesty as he could. And when he told her he suspected her to be at least ten weeks along in her pregnancy, if not slightly more, Meredith crumpled into him. Her slim shoulders heaved with her every grateful sob and she clutched the front of his shirt. Ian simply hugged his friend to him as her joyful tears soaked through the fabric. He held her close and allowed her to feel it all.

What Meredith didn't know was that Ian and her husband had had a few late-night meetings of their own. At first, the viscount had asked if there was anything he, as her husband, could do to help Meredith. It had taken an enormous amount of humility for Sommerfeld to approach him about this, but Ian supposed it was another mark in favor of the man's deep, abiding love for Meredith. Unfortunately, there was little advice Ian could provide that he hadn't already passed along to Meredith. Fertility was, as yet, something medicine seemed incapable of grasping fully.

The latest meeting with the viscount had shifted at one point to a subject Ian had long considered broaching. It was a surgical repair of the viscount's injured leg, but it would involve re-breaking the limb and carried the risk of leaving him with even less mobility than he currently had. Sommerfeld had balked and stormed out, and Ian chose to leave things as they were; the man didn't need any other reasons to dislike him. Perhaps, in his own time and after he realized the physicality of raising a child, the viscount might change his mind.

"There now," Ian murmured, chafing Meredith's back with his broad palms. He was happy for her—really, he was—but he also wanted to remain realistic about the situation. She'd yet to conceive to their knowledge and this might place this pregnancy in a precarious state. Her body had yet to prove it could successfully carry a child. Meredith sat back and swiped at her eyes with a handkerchief she pulled from a pocket in her skirts. "I'm pleased for you, Meredith. Truly, I am. I know how long you've wished for this." She rewarded him with a grateful, watery smile. She'd wanted nothing more than to have her biggest dream fulfilled and it was obvious that she'd worried about how it would hurt him. Her kind and thoughtful heart was one of the reasons he'd proposed to her four years prior. "But you must take it easy in these precarious early weeks."

She nodded. "Of course." If anyone understood the subtext, it was the woman who had stood beside him as they'd absorbed her uncle's medical lessons and lectures.

He scribbled some notes on a piece of parchment for her and fixed a pouch of ginger root for her to chew if nausea began to trouble her in the mornings. "Let me know if you are concerned about anything at all," he said as he presented the items to her, but he held onto them when she would have plucked them from his fingers. "But promise you'll send word next time instead of traversing the streets in the dead of night without your husband to see you arrive safely."

She gave a little laugh and agreed as she tucked the paper and packet into her pocket.

"Thank you, Ian," she said as he walked her to the back door.

"Of course."

"I know this can't have been easy for you—"

"Think nothing of it," he interrupted her and meant it. "I'd far prefer you seek out my care than place yourself in the hands of another physician.

Meredith smiled and squeezed his hand. "My uncle would be so proud of the man you have become."

Ian squeezed her hand back, feeling only the warm camaraderie of decades of friendship.

"And I know he'd be quite proud of how you saved a young woman from being crushed beneath the wheels of a cart." There was a mischievous glint in her indigo eyes. Ian tensed, immediately knowing exactly to whom she was referring. He hadn't stopped thinking about that woman since he'd left her Townhouse the prior week.

"I did nothing heroic," he replied, attempting to affect a nonchalant persona even though a part of him itched to know what Meredith would say about Lady Juliette. Unfortunately, Meredith knew him too well to fall for it.

"Don't worry; you made quite the impression upon her as well." She patted his upper arm and flipped her hood back over her head. Her words left Ian baffled. There was no possibility that he'd left more of an "impression" upon Lady Juliette than she had on him with her impressive mind, bewitching eyes, and lips made to be kissed. He'd had far too many quiet hours to ponder the last. "You are still attending our supper on Friday, correct?" The abrupt topic shift confused him, but he nodded in agreement. "I believe Lady Juliette and the earl will be in attendance as well." The warring emotions inside of Ian made him more than a little uncomfortable. He was excited by the prospect of seeing her once more, as well as the roiling pragmatism that he could never have her. Ian didn't quite know how to respond. Meredith, however, knew precisely what to do: She played to the physician he was.

"At the minimum, it wouldn't hurt to look in on your patient. We should ensure Lady Juliette doesn't overtax herself after her injury."

Ian, finally fully understanding what was going on, looked heavenward for strength before replying. "I will attend for you, but the last thing I need is anyone playing at Matchmaker." Meredith opened her mouth to protest, but he cut her off. "May I see you home?"

"Thank you, no. I am quite safe in the carriage and it's not all that far."

He saw her off and, as the carriage continued down the alley to the main street, he ducked back into his home to re-bolt the door. He set about tidying and cleaning all over again, making sure all the locks were secured once more (twice), and finally ascended the stairs to his bedchamber.

As he lay atop the cold mattress, Ian was surprised to realize that he wasn't as tortured by the thought of Meredith carrying another man's child as he thought he might once have been. Instead, he pondered new foreign phrases with which to challenge Lady Juliette.

Chapter Five

Dinner at the Sommerfeld residence was a smashing success…other than the fact that the earl watched his sister with hawkeyed intensity, affording little opportunity for Ian to speak with her. That, coupled with the thinly-veiled animosity and brusque treatment from the viscount meant dinner was a real treat for Ian.

When he'd arrived, Meredith had pulled him aside and begged him not to mention the pregnancy to her husband just yet. Ian wished she had already done so because perhaps then the glowering man might have been a smidge more tolerable.

After dinner, Ian and the other men retired for drinks and cigars. While Ian could appreciate a good, stiff drink, he did not enjoy smoking and desperately needed space from feeling as if he was the odd man out—to be fair, he was the only man in attendance without a title, so he *was* the odd man out. Ian excused himself from the study and slipped out onto the balcony spanning the rear of the house and overlooking the small, well-kept garden. The address was still situated on a fashionable street, but far enough from Aldborough House and the viscount's parents that Lord and Lady Sommerfeld had privacy and freedom in the early years of their marriage.

Ian leaned against the carved stone railing and inhaled the thick London night air. He loved his profession, he enjoyed healing and spreading his medical knowledge, but there were times when he missed the Highlands of his childhood; the white-capped mountains, rolling fields of purple heather undulating in the wind, the crisp air carrying with it the bleating of sheep and whistles of their shepherds.

A small coo off to the side drew Ian's attention away from the night. Lady Juliette. And she was staring back at him with those glorious eyes, her arms clasped in front of her in a tantalizingly shy, tentative stance. Ever since Meredith's late-night visit to his offices, he'd been unable to think of almost nothing other than seeing the dark-haired young lady, though he'd never admit it.

His stomach flipped. His pulse stuttered.

She truly was uncommonly pretty, Lady Juliette; like a porcelain doll…not meant for a Scottish physician with rough hands and a questionable past.

She had been crafted to be some wealthy lord's pride and joy.

Her gentle smile caused his body to betray itself. And when she stepped closer to join him in the shadows between the doors of the study and parlor, his heart sped up every inch she grew closer. He furiously schooled his features to remain calm despite this.

"Lady Juliette," he greeted her, though his voice came out hoarser than he'd intended. "How does your leg fare? You seem to be moving quite well."

She rewarded him with an even broader smile. "Much better, thank you. I believe this is to be attributed to the fact that I have a somewhat decent physician." Ian couldn't help but chuckle at her cheek. "May I ask why you are outside?"

"I could ask the same of you."

"I felt like taking some air." Her matter-of-fact reply and little shrug of her shoulders were endearing. Perhaps that was why he spoke the truth when he responded to her query.

"No matter how many dinners, balls, and parties I'm invited to, I still feel out of place."

"Whyever is that?" she asked and leaned against the railing beside him, so close he caught a tantalizing hint of her light perfume, a hint of heaven. Her eyes softened in concern and he smiled gently.

"Because I'll never be one of them." *One of you...* It could have been a trick of the light, but he thought he witnessed a gleam of sadness in her eyes. He quickly cleared his throat and changed the subject; "Have you had any luck translating the phrase I gave you?" She shook her head, the light catching in the diamond studs in her ears and wound around her delicate throat. He nodded knowingly in reply. "There isn't much of a market for the language of the Highlands."

"Is that where you spent your childhood?" she inquired, tilting her head in the most charming of manners.

"It was."

"Will you speak more of it, please? So I can hear it again as it is supposed to sound from a native speaker? I always prefer lessons from one born speaking the language than someone who had to learn it, themselves."

At first, Ian thought she might be mocking him, but that was dashed in an instant as he saw the sweet, innocent candor in her eyes. She certainly hadn't been jesting when she'd said she loved languages.

"*Tha thu a' coimhead àlainn a-nochd,*" he spoke softly, the words rolling off his tongue and caressing his lips with the old familiarity of a childhood home.

She made her best approximation of the words and sounds but failed miserably. Rather than become disheartened, she laughed with the lightheartedness of someone who loved life and learning. "What did you say?"

"'You look lovely tonight,'" he replied, his heart kicking up as an unmistakable blush crested her cheeks. He waited to see if she would take offense; instead, she asked in a voice barely above a whisper for another phrase.

"*Tha d' inntinn na iongnadh,*" he murmured. An unbidden heat began to pool in his loins.

Again, Lady Juliette tried her best to mimic the vowels and consonants. Though he did his best to disguise it with a cough, he couldn't help a small chuckle at her clumsy efforts. "You are mocking me!" she hissed and swatted his arm playfully.

"Do not worry," he reassured her, capturing her gloved hand in his, wishing he could feel the warmth of the soft skin beneath the satin. "No matter how good an ear you have, it is no easy language—especially not for a *Sassenach* who hasn't heard its like before."

"*Sassenach*?" She frowned. "What did you just call me?"

"'English,'" he replied with a tilt of his lips.

"And before that? What was that phrase?"

"'Your mind is a wonder.'"

She looked down to where he still held her hand in his, her long ebony lashes shielding her eyes from him. He knew he should release her, every fiber of his common sense told him to do so, but she didn't seem to mind. She shuffled another step closer to him and met his eyes once more.

"Teach me something simple." There was no denying her anything when she looked up at him like that. "How do I say, 'My name is Juliette'?"

"'*S e Juliette an t-ainm a th'orm*," he translated and then proceeded to guide her through every sound with deliberate slowness. He explained how to move her lips and tongue to form the unfamiliar words. It felt unexpectedly relieving to be speaking like this to a woman. The rest of the world melted away and he could almost believe she accepted him just as he was at his soul.

She was innocent.

She was naive.

And Ian would be damned if he knew what drew him to her like some ill-fated moth to the deadliest of flames. The way she watched his lips as he spoke; the way, as she leaned closer to better hear his hushed tone and pronunciation, he could feel the warmth of her body, drove him mad.

So mad, in fact, that Ian closed the gap between them and captured Lady Juliette's mouth with his own.

She released a startled squeak and stiffened.

And Ian knew he'd just destroyed his entire career, his life, for an idiotic impulse. And that realization would forever color this moment in his memory.

He tore himself away from her petal-soft lips and released her to stumble backward several steps. It still didn't feel like a safe enough distance. His heartbeat was deafeningly loud in his ears as the organ hammered against the inside of his ribcage. He opened his mouth to speak, but no words came out. Not even a pitiful sound.

Lady Juliette looked nothing short of dazed and confused.

Until she closed the gap between them and Ian braced himself for the slap he knew was coming. She raised her gloved hand and…

cupped his cheek a moment before her fingers slid back to the nape of his neck to tangle in his hair. She stood on the tips of her toes and pulled Ian's head down to meet hers once more.

Their lips met and Ian groaned at her taste, freely given. She was sweet and tentative, obviously unskilled, but he didn't think he could have possibly enjoyed the kiss more.

He rested a hand at her waist just before the point where it swelled to the delicate slope of her hip; his other hand moved beneath her chin and a crooked finger gently tilted her head. He guided her and, as he suspected, she was a ready pupil. He traced the seam of her lips with his tongue and she sighed, leaning further into his arms. He could have gladly kissed her for hours, but a burst of masculine laughter seeped through the cracked door leading back into the study. Ian and Lady Juliette flew apart as if by electrical shock, both their chests heaving.

He was tortured by the dazed look in her eyes and the fingertips she pressed to her rosy, petal-soft lips.

"I...no one has ever done that to me before..." she murmured, though he could not be sure if it was to him or more to herself. Even in the shadows, he could see the bright pink coloring on the soft apples of her cheeks.

"My sincerest apologies, Lady Juliette." Ian tried to sound contrite, but a twisted part of him enjoyed the fact that she would always remember him as her first kiss; he would have this part of her even as she went on to marry a great lord and bear his children. "I should not have taken such liberties with your person." She quickly shook her head and held up her hand to forestall any further apologies from him.

"I should thank you." This stunned Ian into utter silence; his mouth snapped shut in shock. "I admit I'd been rather curious about what it would be like to be kissed...and to kiss...and now I don't have to

wonder anymore." Surely Ian couldn't believe his ears? It took everything in him not to pull her to him once more and plunder her mouth
like a feral beast. "My brother usually keeps such a careful eye on me,
I'm not usually allowed into a situation where this might occur." She
began to ramble and then caught herself. "So, I suppose, I am trying
to thank you. For the enlightenment. Again."

She then quickly ducked back into the doorway to the parlor, the
edge of her skirts disappearing just as the earl came out onto the ve-
randa to find a very bemused Ian staring toward her retreat.

Juliette returned to the parlor, her pounding heart deafening in her
ears. She commended herself on handling her recent interaction with
such decorum and nonchalance when her knees and insides felt less
substantial than an undercooked pudding. She could scarcely believe
Dr. McCullom had kissed her, and it took everything in her power to
not draw attention to it by pressing her fingers to her tingling lips.
He'd tasted of warmed brandy and honey. Sweet and seductively sensual.

"You look a little piqued, dear," Lady Sommerfeld took notice of
her return and addressed her from the sofa. "Are you well?"

Not trusting her voice, Juliette could only nod and cast down her
gaze to her trembling fingers.

There was a slight pause before the viscountess spoke again. "The
men should be joining us shortly for cards."

Juliette's head snapped up. She wasn't sure she could face Dr.
McCullom just yet; or her brother, for that matter. She could feel her
cheeks warming and silently prayed it would stop before it became
too obvious. Before she could pluck a decent response from her jum-
bled mind, Lady Sommerfeld leaned her red head close to Juliette's
and spoke in a quiet, reassuring tone, placing a conspiratorial hand

over Juliette's trembling one to steady it. "I promise not to tell if you won't…as long as you don't get up to too much mischief."

Juliette rapidly shook her head in denial. "I don't—that is…I am not—"

"Calm yourself," Lady Sommerfeld whispered and smiled warmly, remarkably adept at disguising her words with a benign presentation. "Both you and I were raised in similar restrictive situations. Think of this as the opportunity to have the exciting, flirtatious girlhood we never had." She nudged her shoulder against Juliette's. "And what is youth without a little intrigue and forbidden romance?" Juliette's cheeks flared an even deeper shade of crimson, but an incorrigible smile tugged at the corners of her mouth. "I promise to feign ignorance if your brother catches wind of anything and set him on another path. Just promise me you will be cautious; there is no harm in some stolen kisses with an honorable man, so long as you are smart about it and careful not to lose your head."

Juliette could only squeeze her friend's hand in return. She didn't know whether to be grateful or mortified that she had so easily guessed what had transpired on the balcony, but she had to admit that it felt rather nice to have the support. A coconspirator.

True to Lady Sommerfeld's word, the men joined the ladies in the parlor shortly thereafter. Juliette offered Ian a shy smile as he trailed in behind her brother and Viscount Sommerfeld with his cane, but his eyes danced over her as if she was no more important than another piece of furniture.

This continued throughout the rest of the evening and the games of whist Lady Sommerfeld seemed incapable of losing. While the undercurrent of competitiveness between their hosts was amusing and entertaining, Juliette couldn't stop her eyes from continually darting over to Dr. McCullom. He was so handsome in his dark coat and starched white cravat. Despite his impeccable manners and cultured speech, there was still something half-tamed about him; and Juliette thought she may have gotten just a taste of it out on the balcony.

"I am finished!" announced the viscount. "She's already tripled her pin money for the month and my ego can take no further bruising." His words were exasperated, but there was mirth in there and it was echoed back in Lady Sommerfeld's deep blue eyes.

"You knew what you were getting into when you suggested cards, darling." She proceeded to shuffle the cards with a finesse Juliette had never witnessed.

"Another hand or two," Ethan interjected. "The night is young and it would appear I've not learned my lesson."

"Nor I," announced the Duchess of Morton, an impressive flare of determination in her eyes. "I cannot leave this house without having won a single hand."

Lady Sommerfeld laughed airly and looked at her other guests. "Lady Juliette? Dr. McCullom? Shall I deal you in for this round? Or would you perhaps prefer a game of chess?" She gestured to the far corner of the room where a carved marble board had been laid out.

Juliette quickly found herself seated across from Dr. McCullom, facing him over the chessboard. She played white and he, black, though her heart was not in the game. Every time she looked up, Dr. McCullom's eyes refused to meet hers, though, internally, she commanded him to so much as hold her gaze for even three seconds. She desperately wanted to see how he would react to her nearness in the light. Would his breathing quicken as hers did? Would he watch her lips as they formed her words? Would his desire be as raw as she'd felt on the balcony?

Alas, he seemed intent upon steering their conversation to every inane topic known to mankind. She moved a pawn and he inquired after her ankle; he moved a rook and they chatted about the weather—anything to keep clear of what had happened between them on the balcony. Not that she wanted to discuss it within earshot of her brother…she didn't know what, exactly she wanted, but it certainly wasn't this coolness; it was in such stark contrast to the man who'd held her and kissed her in the dark! She didn't know what she expected, either. It was just one kiss, after all. And Dr. McCullom was a virile, handsome, intelligent man with an excellent profession. He likely kissed women all the time.

But, maybe, she'd hoped for a hint that he'd felt even a modicum of the tremors she had…that she still felt.

Juliette's mood turned darker with every move of the pieces across the board. She played recklessly and foolishly, losing one piece after another.

"You don't play much chess, then, I take it?" Dr. McCullom said beneath his breath as he swiped away her rook in a move a child could have seen coming.

"I play a fair bit," she ground out as pleasantly as possible. She slid her bishop several spaces.

"Unless you are luring me into an extremely deep false sense of security—which I highly doubt at this point—I don't see much finesse on this playing field." His words were aggravatingly lighthearted.

She nearly growled when he claimed another of her pieces. Even at that moment, she recognized how childish her turn in moods was, but there was simply no stopping it. "A true gentleman would hardly make such a comment when playing with a lady," she finally snapped.

Dr. McCullom sat back in his chair as if her words had been a physical strike. Indeed, she must have spoken louder than intended because even the card game had paused and the room fell silent. Juliette flinched in shame when she realized how, not only were all eyes upon her, but there was a well-masked stricken glint to Dr. McCullom's gaze and a tautness of his well-formed mouth.

Lady Sommerfeld's mouth was agape; Ethan eyed them with hawklike interest, his body tense as he decided whether he needed to intervene.

She fully recognized that she had no reason to be snippy with Dr. McCullom. She'd likely given the poor man whiplash from the speed with which she'd gone from boldly thanking him for her first kiss to her irritation that it didn't appear to have meant as much to him as it did to her.

Dr. McCullom's expression and tone remained cool, though he raised a perplexed chestnut brow.

"I—I am sor—" she began to stammer a quick apology until the doctor cut her off.

"I apologize if I have offended you in any way, Lady Juliette," he said, low enough for her ears only. "I seem to have misjudged the situation." He stood and knocked over his king with the knuckle of his longest finger, signaling his forfeiture of the game with a final snap of marble-on-marble. She stared at the fallen piece on the board as it rocked back and forth on its polished side. From the corner of her eye, she saw Dr. McCullom sketch her a proper bow, pivot on his heel, and heard him make his excuses to the rest of their party. He claimed he had many appointments the following morning and really should be going.

Every clipped footstep taking him further from only deepened Juliette's terrible mortification and guilt.

Chapter Six

The next day, Ian returned to his offices for a late dinner after having spent his morning making house calls. His day had been filled with two cases of indigestion, one severe bout of gout, the laborious task of setting a lad's broken arm after he'd been thrown by a horse, and looking in on a patient with dropsy. And he was worn out. His hollow stomach growled in agreement. Unfortunately, his schedule was not conducive to a man of his size and stature; he could have easily eaten twice as much as he normally did and still experience some hunger pangs, but he'd long ago learned to work through the discomfort. Keeping his mind and his hands occupied went a long way to that end.

Entering through the front door, he quickly descended the stairs to the lower level. The enticing scent of one of Mrs. Brown's hearty stews grew stronger with every step. Ian's mouth was watering by the time he popped his head into the warm kitchen and found the woman using her apron to fan the steam from a fresh loaf of crusty golden bread. The pot hanging in the hearth bubbled away merrily, calling to Ian with every pop and squeak.

"Smells divine, Mrs. Brown," he said by way of greeting.

"Get on to your office now," she shooed him away with a smile. "I'll bring a bowl to you shortly; I know how busy you are and how little time you make for eating."

Ian nodded, allowing her to fuss and grumble about his habits as he made his way down the hall, through the exam room, and to his private office. He quickly shrugged off his coat and draped it over the chair before sitting down. The tap of footsteps told him his lunch was imminent and he made quick work of clearing his papers to create room for the food. He'd learned long ago the hierarchy in Mrs. Brown's mind: strictly food and then work. More than a few of his papers in the early days had been smudged by food being served atop them.

"What good is work if your belly growls so loud you cannot think?" she'd harrumphed at him time and time again.

A space was cleared just in time for Mrs. Brown to deposit a tin plate carrying thick slices of fresh bread and a hearty bowl of what appeared to be a mutton stew with a variety of root vegetables swimming in a thick, decadent gravy. The fare would not be served at any dinner parties, but, as far as Ian was concerned, it was more delicious than most. It was like a taste of home—something his mother would have made.

"Thank you, Mrs. Brown," he said sincerely, already picking up his spoon to dive into the meal. His eyes began to skim the top paper of the stack beside the bowl. The post had arrived and a thick pile of envelopes awaited his attention. He likely wouldn't make it through all of them before he had to leave for his next appointment, but he could at least begin the job. Perhaps he'd sleep that night at a reasonable hour.

He'd only made it through two bites of the delicious stew before the bell on the back door broke the silence.

He heard Mrs. Brown stop her washing up and stride over to answer the caller. The door was normally unlocked during business hours when Ian was home, but she'd taken to locking it for a brief period of the day to allow him time to eat. She'd taken on the role of unofficial gatekeeper.

All the doors on the lower level were open, so he didn't have to strain his hearing to listen as Mrs. Brown advised that he was not currently seeing patients, but, if they left a card and a message, she would make sure he received it.

"Oh, I am not here for medical care…it is regarding a matter more personal in nature." Ian could just make out the words, but they were slightly muffled. There were several more exchanges between Mrs. Brown and the persistent caller until Ian popped a bite of bread in his mouth, stood to brush crumbs from his hands, and sighed. Clearly, this caller was not taking no for an answer.

It wouldn't be the first time a lady had been so bold as to sneak into his office hoping for a private assignation of a more intimate nature.

He didn't bother to don his coat and strode through the office and back up the hallway where Mrs. Brown held the door only half open, blocking the gap with her body.

"My apologies, miss. As I said before, Dr. McCullom is not currently accepting callers."

"Please—"

"It's alright, Mrs. Brown," Ian cut off the unseen caller and wrapped his fingers around the door. His housekeeper didn't like it, but she nodded her head and ducked back into the kitchen to leave him to handle the situation. When Ian opened the door all the way, however, he wasn't prepared for who awaited him.

Lady Juliette's lips parted in surprise and then relief when he appeared in the doorframe.

Ian was not a man who enjoyed drama. He preferred a quiet existence with as little trouble as possible. If the past few weeks—especially the last twenty-four hours—had taught him anything, it was that Lady Juliette was trouble. She represented about a dozen manifestations of it for him, not the least of which was her showing up at his offices and, thanks to a glance, unescorted by her brother. Only a meek little maid fidgeted off to the side, clearly worried her employer would sack her as soon he discovered where she'd allowed his sister to slip off to.

After the way Lady Juliette had spoken to him the previous night, Ian had half a mind to allow Mrs. Brown to have her way and toss out the young woman. He might have understood her behavior if she'd been insulted or offended by his behavior on the balcony. But, if he'd offended Lady Juliette with his kisses, then why the bloody hell had she *thanked* him for it? It made absolutely no sense to Ian's logical mind…and her appearance on his doorstep could spell only trouble for him.

It had taken every last ounce of his willpower to remain composed when he and the other men had rejoined the ladies in the parlor for games. Seeing the faint blush on her porcelain cheeks, catching her watching him from beneath those long coal-colored lashes of hers, witnessing the unsteady rise and fall of her breasts above the edge of her honey-yellow gown was disconcerting in the most tantalizing of ways. Lest he give himself away, he'd opted for intense civility and strict adherence to propriety. That was until he'd had the chance to spend some time with her relatively one-on-one at the chessboard. Her outburst had startled him, to say the least. But Ian was a man who had long ago learned when his presence did more harm than good. It was safer to take his leave and allow Lady Juliette to have her feelings than risk it all coming out in front of her brother. The earl had the eyes and—Ian suspected—the talons of a hawk; especially when it came to his twin sister.

Fingers tightening on the door, Ian opened his mouth to turn Lady Juliette away, but no sound came out when her eyes met his. Something stopped him—whether the memory of her taste and touch, or simple manners—and he opened the door more widely, gesturing for her to enter.

"Thank you," she whispered, suddenly far more bashful than she'd been when pleading with Mrs. Brown to grant her entrance. The nervous little maid slipped in behind her and the door was latched once again.

"To what do I owe this visit, Lady Juliette?" he asked, cocking a curious brow. She glanced between her maid and Mrs. Brown where she stood at the kitchen table, watching with her hands on her ample hips—a formidable little gargoyle in a mobcap.

"Might we speak in your office?"

Ian had half a mind to make her say whatever it was with their audience, but, after a tense moment, he gestured for her to lead the way down the hall and into his treatment room. She told her maid to wait in one of the chairs that lined the hallway. Rather than stop, he showed Lady Juliette to his study where his repast still awaited him. He stared longingly at the food growing cold there on his desk, but it would have been rude to eat in front of her. Then again, he should have donned his coat before seeing her, so it was rather a wash. The minutes were ticking by, bringing him ever closer to when he would have to leave for his next appointment…full belly or not.

Rather than sit in the chair he hastily cleared off for her, Lady Juliette slowly perused the small space. Every available surface was covered with papers and books, medical instruments and correspondence. As meticulously clean as the rest of his offices were, this one space resembled his mind and its many directions and layers. Despite its fullness, the room was relatively well-organized. His eyes tracked Lady Juliette as she took in the neat stacks of files, the books and meticulously categorized notebooks, and even a human skull. Much to his surprise, she seemed fascinated by the artifact and even reached out to touch the smooth, knitted crest of the cranium.

Ian cleared his throat. "Please, have a seat," he said, gesturing to the chair.

She did as he asked, smoothing her blush-colored skirts around her legs. He tried not to ponder just how long and shapely those legs were beneath the layers of fabric.

Her eyes caught the food on his desk and her face unexpectedly melted into one of concern. "Oh! I've interrupted your luncheon!"

She had, but Ian was too much of a gentleman to admit to the inconvenience. He waved off her concern and sat across from her. "Now, what can I help you with?"

She lowered her gaze once more where her fingers toyed with an embroidered rosette on her skirts. "I—I need to apologize. For my behavior last night. It was unkind and unfair of me." Ian sat back in the chair, waiting to see if she would continue. The pink tint to her cheeks made his heart stutter. "I admit it was silly of me to get upset when you appeared so nonplussed by our…by what we shared on the balcony while I was so flustered." Her words continued to pour forth in a torrent and Ian listened, hardly believing his ears. Her mesmerizing eyes met his once more. "I realize I shouldn't have held it against you—no doubt you found my abilities mediocre at best, thanks to my inexperience." Her cheeks flared an even deeper shade of pink. "So how can I possibly blame you for being unmoved?"

Fighting back an amused grin, Ian held up his hand to stave off any further verbal onslaught. Her face was fairly aflame at that point, and he didn't want her to combust spontaneously.

He eyed her for a moment before speaking. "I accept your apology." She rewarded him with a bashful, if grateful, smile. "But you are sorely mistaken if you believe I was unmoved by the kiss." Her wide eyes flew to his.

"Well, you're certainly a fair actor," she whispered.

Ian finally set his smile free. "Not a good actor, merely old enough and wise enough to hide how I feel when I have just kissed the beloved sister of an overly protective peer of the Realm. I do enjoy my job, after all…and *breathing*." She rewarded him with a breathy laugh that caused chills to tickle every inch of his spine.

"I suppose it was a wise decision." She said before rifling through the reticule strapped to her wrist and retrieving a small notebook. "There wasn't the opportunity to tell you last night, but I managed to translate the first phrase you gave me, but the way." The pride on her face was enchanting.

"Oh?" Ian sat back in his chair, recalling vividly the first Gaelic challenge he'd issued. It had been foolish to say such a thing to her, but he hadn't been able to help himself.

"Tha mi a' guidhe gun stadadh an saoghal a' tionndadh agus mar sin cha tàinig am mionaid seo gu crìch." Lady Juliette pronounced the words passably, halting only occasionally around a particularly foreign combination of sounds. "'I wish the world would stop turning so

this moment never ended.'" A pregnant silence followed, their eyes never breaking contact. "Did you mean that?"

The truth was, he had. Being near her made him reckless, but it also nourished his soul like nothing else had in years. She warmed a part of him that had grown jaded and tired.

It was Ian's turn to flush uncomfortably. He nodded once in reply.

"It's lovely," she breathed, and he was inordinately pleased she thought so.

"*Tha thu nad bhoireannach gun choimeas ann am bòidhchead agus tuigse,*" he said impulsively. *You are a woman unmatched in beauty and intelligence.* She eagerly accepted the challenge and scribbled the phrase with a pencil in her little notebook, asking him to repeat it several times for her.

"I wish I could have someone teach me the language; half the fun of it is learning the nuances native speakers use. Tutors for the other languages I know weren't all that hard to come by. Your Gaelic, on the other hand…"

Ian barely stopped himself in time before he offered to fill the position himself; the more rational side of his brain kicked in to save him. He was busy enough with his actual profession and there were not enough hours in the day to eat a proper meal, let alone play at tutor… not to mention that to do so would place him in the foolishly dangerous situation where he would invariably grow closer with this intoxicating beauty. He enjoyed and appreciated her earnest desire to learn, the mesmerizing glitter in her eyes as she hung on his every word. It would be far too easy for him to forget who she was—who he was…

"I will make some inquiries on your behalf," he offered and then changed the subject. "However did you get free of the earl's watchful eye?"

She leaned in and spoke in a conspiratorial tone so her maid would not hear her through the doors left ajar. "I told him I needed to finish shopping since my last trip was interrupted. If asked—which I have no doubt she will be—my maid will have nothing else to offer other than my ankle began to trouble me with all the walking and we needed to retrieve more of your miracle pain powder here at your offices."

Ian smiled in response to her cunning and then glanced at his timepiece, realizing he needed to head off to his next appointment. "While I appreciate the visit and the apology, Lady Juliette, I'm afraid I must be off." He tried not to read too much into her crestfallen expression as he picked up his coat and slipped it on.

Juliette watched Dr. McCullom don his coat, Lady Sommerfeld's words echoing around in her skull alongside the conversation she'd just shared with the physician standing before her. She steeled her resolve and clenched her hands to bolster her bravery, hoping her expression was one of coy confidence.

"I suppose I will have to continue to find myself in odd predicaments if I desire to see you again."

Dr. McCullom froze with only one arm in his sleeve. After a moment of stillness, he spoke and moved at the pace of molasses.

"I don't believe that would be a good idea."

"And I don't see why not; besides, I don't view you as a man who would leave one's education lacking." She gestured to the framed certificates, diplomas, and awards lining the walls of his offices.

"Education?" There was something unbearably charming about the two vertical slices appearing between his brows as he frowned.

"Why, kissing, of course." He nearly choked on the breath in his lungs, but she continued determinedly. She'd already begun and that was the hardest part, wasn't it? "If last night proved one thing to me, it is that I am sorely underprepared in that field. I don't care to feel that way, and this is perhaps the only area of my life my brother cannot fix by hiring an expensive tutor."

Thank God, thought Ian, still somewhat unsure of the reality of what he was hearing. Surely Lady Juliette could not be serious? This must surely be some cruel joke women of breeding played upon men in service they found passably attractive. Ian had been propositioned many times under a variety of circumstances, but never anything such as this.

"You said so yourself that you found the kiss enjoyable, so it stands to reason this wouldn't be a hardship for you," Lady Juliette continued with the lift of one shoulder.

He scoffed in disbelief before making several unintelligible sounds. There simply were no words available in his vocabulary to respond to the situation.

"I've had so little freedom and excitement in my life." Her tone was painfully soft, almost pleading. "Could you possibly deny me this? What harm could there be in it?"

"What harm?" Ian croaked out. Did she believe him to be as weak and harmless as a kitten? Was she so sheltered that she didn't realize what he could do to her? What he really wanted from her? The thoughts that kept him throbbing and aching awake every night since the day he'd met her?

He rounded the desk in only a couple of steps to tower over Lady Juliette. His already frantic pulse increased when he caught the light scent of her perfume. If only she knew how he longed to bury his face in her neck, between her pale breasts and bathe in her unique aroma.

"What harm?" he asked again, lower instead of louder, a part of him still realizing there were others not all that far away.

Her instincts seemed to kick in and she stood so she was at less of an advantage. Ian stepped closer, backing her up against his desk, forcing her with his height to lean back and brace her hands on the desktop to look up into his face.

"It would be very dangerous, indeed," he all but growled. "What your self-proclaimed ignorance cannot comprehend is that kissing you would only inevitably make any man want *more*."

Chapter Seven

Dr. McCullom towered over Juliette, his accent becoming thick as treacle—something she hadn't heard before from him. It seemed he dampened it here in England to make his English patients more comfortable.

She quite liked it.

It made her uncomfortable in a delicious way.

Juliette tilted her head defiantly, meeting his dilated eyes with hers, hoping he wouldn't notice the birdlike frenetic pulse in her throat. "I'll have to trust your comportment as a gentleman."

His mouth tilted in the most wicked of smiles. "Has anyone told you, lass, that Scotsmen aren't gentlemen, but savages?" His mouth immediately covered hers in a bruising kiss of possession. If she'd enjoyed their kiss the prior night, it was nothing compared to what this entirely new version made her feel. Gone was the tentative touch, the unsure reception…in its place was a strength and desire unlike any other.

His tongue swept against the seam of her lips; his teeth nibbled the fullness of her bottom lip. She parted her lips with a sigh, granting him access. He changed the angle and their teeth clicked, their lips met and parted, his tongue dove in to duel with her inexperienced one. She had to grip the edge of the desk behind her to keep her knees from buckling. She'd never thought...never imagined it could be like this. He set an unfamiliar fire beneath her skin until every inch of her burned to be closer to him, to have his hands exploring and teasing the rest of her just as his mouth was. She longed to arch her body and press her tingling breasts to the broad, hard wall of his chest. She wanted to feel more.

More.

More.

When he finally tore his mouth away, he pressed his forehead to hers, his broad shoulders heaving with every panting breath. He whispered in a voice as rough as granite, "You clearly have no idea of the dangerous game you are playing, and in which you are asking me to take part." Juliette's mind moved sluggishly and, by the time it had caught up to his words, he'd already retreated several paces to adjust his hair and his jacket. And he stepped from the room.

Still, on weakened legs, Juliette followed him back into the exam room to find him, head hanging, bracing his palms atop his apothecary table with its many nooks and crannies. His broad back was to her and it undulated with his every heavy breath.

The silence stretched on. She was about to ask him if he was unwell, but he straightened and began plucking items from the shelves. He deftly prepared a packet with practiced hands for her and held it out.

She stared dumbly at it until he spoke.

"It is the pain powder you claimed to be visiting me to retrieve," he explained flatly, still not quite meeting her eyes. "It wouldn't do to return without it."

Pulling her lower lip between her teeth, Juliette nodded and accepted the packet, shoving it into her reticule. She wasn't prepared for him to close the gap between them so he could tuck a loose curl behind her ear with his large, surprisingly dextrous hand. His finger lingering upon her cheek loosed a shiver throughout her body and her eyelids fluttered with her breath.

"Do not misunderstand me this time. I am declining not because I don't find your proposition bloody appealing, but because you are not for me."

Juliette cocked a brow. "Don't be such a martyr under the guise of righteousness." His eyes widened. Honestly, she was just as surprised that such bold words snuck past her lips. "I may be inexperienced, but I am not stupid. I know you want to say yes. And only an idiot would turn down a no-strings-attached offer of something he desired. You don't strike me as a fool or an idiot, Dr. McCullom." Shock gave way to something in his features Juliette could not name, but that quickly morphed into something she did understand: frustration.

"Are you insinuating that I am an idiot if I do not accept your proposal?" he ground out, barely quiet enough that her maid and his housekeeper wouldn't overhear. The barely-banked fire in his eyes made Juliette second-guess her word choice, but there was no turning back now. For better or for worse, the gauntlet had been thrown. She swallowed hard.

"I am merely stating that to deny what is freely offered—especially when it is something you so clearly desire—is unbelievably irrational for a rational man such as yourself."

He huffed a gruff sigh and ran a hand through his hair, yanking some of the burnished chestnut locks free of their queue. He stared out the street-level window and the passing shadows beyond for several tense minutes before his eyes flew to hers once again.

"Fine," he snapped and his eyes widened as if he couldn't believe the capitulation had come from his mouth. "But let me make this painfully clear: Nothing can come of this. We get out of it what we desire, but you'd best not harbor notions about a more permanent arrangement. There is no room for girlish fantasies." Juliette injected steel into her spine in response.

"I am a spinster of six and twenty, not a debutante. Any fantasies I may have once had died long ago. I merely want to experience a taste of the world within my books while I still can." She delicately cleared the emotion from her throat. "You are my chance, Dr. McCullom. You have met my brother, so you've some idea what I am up against. Teach me."

He eyed her for several more heartbeats, weighing her words, reading the double meaning they held, before he nodded once and gestured toward the door. "And call me Ian," he said in a low tone as she passed by him. Her steps halted and she looked up into his handsome face.

"And, to you, I am Juliette." Her lips tilted into a hesitant smile before she led the way from the exam room and he quickly repaired his hair.

"Continue the dosage as prescribed and send word if you find it does not help." Ian held the door for her as he spoke loudly enough to catch the attention of his housekeeper and her maid. Fanny stood immediately. "Would you please see that the carriage is brought straight to the door for Lady Juliette? She should rest her ankle and not strain herself with any unnecessary travel."

The maid nodded and ducked out as Juliette shot him a glare from beneath her lashes. His statement within earshot of her maid just assured her of a quiet weekend without any activities. The blasted man seemed to know this and enjoy it, given the cocky tilt of his brow.

It was a matter of minutes until he saw her safely into her carriage and she was whisked away back to Hopesend House.

But it wasn't for several hours more before the gravity of what Juliette had accomplished truly set in. She was utterly stunned by her own boldness—she'd never been so daring in her life! Thinking back on it as she sat comfortably in the family sitting room, the entire situation felt like one long fevered dream. A strange, vivid daydream where she could still feel the echo of Ian's kiss upon her lips and taste him on her tongue.

As she halfheartedly worked her piece of embroidery, she wondered at her sheer lack of planning. At the time, she'd believed herself to be cunning and worldly...yet she hadn't even thought of how she and Ian were going to be able to meet again. She silently berated her rash behavior, stabbing her needle through her stitching and piercing her thumb with its sharp point. She yelped, causing Ethan to look up from where he was reading his book in a nearby armchair.

"Are you well?"

"I'm fine," she snapped before sticking her thumb in her mouth, tasting the metallic tang of blood. The puncture continued to bleed, so she wrapped a handkerchief around it and applied pressure. She supposed she deserved that for wielding a needle with little care or thought.

Ethan set aside his book, propping it open on the arm of the chair, and eyed her closely. "You've been uncommonly testy as of late, Jules."

"I know, I'm sorry for that." She sighed and her shoulders slumped. "I don't quite know what's gotten into me." His piercing eyes continued to bore into her. He recognized there was more to it than that. Her twin knew her better than anyone; he'd always been able to tell when something was troubling her, no matter how well she hid it. It had been a connection they'd shared from birth—their mother had called it their "gift."

"You seem restless," Ethan commented. "The Season is nearly over. Perhaps it's time for a change of scenery and some fresh air. We don't have any pressing invitations at the moment, and any of my remaining business can be handled from the country. Perhaps we can retire from London early this year?"

Juliette gave a noncommittal tilt of her head. While it sounded lovely and she loved their family's country home, it meant she would have to miss a couple of their Reading Society meetings…not to mention her plans with Ian would well and truly be over before they'd even begun.

But maybe that was for the best.

Hadn't she just been pondering how clumsy and ill-conceived her plan was? The chance was slim that her brother would approve of her receiving Gaelic lessons from Dr. McCullom, even less that he would allow them to be alone enough for Juliette to achieve the other half of her goal…

Her heart sank a little lower in her breast.

"If you'd like, maybe you can throw together a small house party? I know how you enjoy organizing such things."

The task was usually reserved for the wives of lords, but Ethan was as yet unmarried and, as far as she and anyone else saw, had no hint of an inclination to do so anytime soon. Juliette had happily filled in for this part of the social role of countess ever since it was clear she was not going to be snatched up on the Marriage Mart. She was fully aware that Ethan used it as a way to distract and entertain her since she was usually kept under lock and key. She would be allowed to organize and host such events on his behalf as the pseudo-lady of the household.

And he usually gave her fairly free reign to do as she wished with her plans.

Juliette perked up.

Perhaps this was the answer she needed.

"That sounds like a lovely idea," she replied evenly, keeping her excitement in check. She would spend the next several days plotting away, and, thanks to Dr. McCullom's proclamation that she take additional rest, she had nothing but time.

For his part, Ian lay awake late that evening wondering how in the hell he'd been goaded into agreeing to this farce. Juliette may be young and sheltered, but she was *far* from stupid. It was at once terrifying and exciting.

It was three weeks before Ian heard from Juliette again; he'd actually begun to allow himself to believe she'd come to her senses and abandoned her foolish aim. He should have been pleased that the chit had stopped pursuing him, but there was no denying the pang of disappointment he experienced as day after day passed and it became more of a possibility.

In the meantime, Ian dove back into his work and tried to clear Juliette's eager lips and heady nectar from his memory.

At night, when sleep eluded him, he would work on his passion project—something near and dear to his heart; a goal that he hoped was not too far off. As long as his practice continued to flourish as it already was, with any luck, he'd soon have to consider scouring medical schools for an apprentice. He needed someone with the right schooling, but still malleable enough where he could shape them to his methods and proven practices.

It was late in the evening and Ian was rifling through his files for a particular one when he accidentally knocked over the stack of post Mrs. Brown had left for him. He stooped to pick up the scattered mess and, within the bunch, there was an innocuous-seeming envelope of thick cream paper with elegant, swooping script. Intrigued, he stood and retrieved his penknife to slice it open. Though he recognized the impression in the midnight black seal, he didn't allow his mind to jump to conclusions until his eyes scanned the writing once, twice.

Juliette, on behalf of her brother, the Earl of Hopesend, invited him to a house party in the country. And it was to be a week in duration.

Beneath his thumb at the bottom of the page was a slightly smudged, hasty postscript. There was no doubt as to its author.

Juliette had issued him a challenge: *Tha an duais as motha a' leantainn a' chunnart as motha.*

That little minx.

The greatest reward follows the greatest risk.

Ian shook his head. My, but she'd been a busy little nymph.

Chapter Eight

"And you've been feeling well? No nausea or pains?" Ian asked as he picked up his bag.

"Truly, I have not," Meredith replied with a laugh. "The answer was the same five and ten minutes ago." Her elegant features glowed with good cheer and health. She still hadn't told her husband about her pregnancy, which meant Ian had been forced to time his visit while the viscount was meeting with his solicitors. Despite her continued subterfuge, Ian could tell his friend was growing more and more optimistic as time went on. She'd even felt the first flutters of quickening in her womb and they estimated the pregnancy to be nearing twenty weeks along, all very good signs, indeed.

"And you will—"

"Send for you if there is the slightest hint of a problem." She smiled as she finished his sentence for him. They'd done this dance once each week since she'd sought him out at his office that evening one month prior. Ian chuckled and then sobered.

"You know, you are at a point where you could tell Sommerfeld about the pregnancy. I'm sure he would be elated—"

"I know," she cut him off. "I'm just...not quite ready."

Ian nodded but knew full well she didn't have much time left to hold onto her secret. Meredith was a lean woman and her abdomen was finally beginning to show evidence of a swell. It was entirely her decision and he would respect it. Not every physician in his position would defer to a woman's wishes and afford her her privacy—what Ian believed was a wife's right to keep health-related secrets from her husband—but Ian would go to his grave before he broke Meredith's confidence. While she'd reached a less tenuous point in the pregnancy, she'd experienced so much disappointment that he suspected it was difficult for her to speak it into reality and let her husband in. Though it paled in comparison, he'd felt something similar when his application to attend the medical school in Edinburgh had been accepted. He'd stared at the letter every single night for weeks and said nothing to his mother until the morning his classes began and he walked out the door. He knew Meredith would do it in her own time.

"I'll see you next week then."

Ian flipped open his timepiece as he descended the stairs and noted that he had thirty minutes to make it to his next appointment. Conveniently for him, it was also in Mayfair, so he needn't rush. He slipped the clock back into his pocket and looked up once more to find a beaming Lady Juliette standing in the foyer.

His heart did a powerful flip when confronted with her beautiful face, the kissable pillows of her lips, the earnest glitter in her eyes. She wore a lilac walking dress and matching pelisse with embroidered frog closures and buttons. The contrast with her pale skin and dark hair was striking and, Ian thought, quite stunningly beautiful.

"Juliette." He greeted her with a tilt to his head, his deep tone hinting at the slightly deeper intimacy they shared. The slight flush to her cheeks indicated she'd caught onto it. He saw her eyes flit to the case in his hand and then back to his face. The sudden loss of pallor alarmed him to the point where he hastily set his bag on the floor and rushed to steady her with a hand upon her elbow.

"Is Lady Sommerfeld ill? Has something happened?" She grabbed his hand, her tiny gloved one dwarfed by his. He tried not to look too much into the fact that she not only accepted his support but sought his comfort.

"All is well, just some fatigue," he gently reassured her. He had become used to this reaction when he was found visiting a home. People often assumed the worst when a physician was called. Her shoulders sagged slightly, drawing his eyes downward to see that she held a large cream-colored envelope, much like the one in which his invitation to her house party had arrived. He tilted his chin in its direction.

"You know, the post usually delivers itself."

It took Juliette a moment to read the teasing tilt to Ian's mouth. "Oh! I was just passing by and I had intended to visit Lady Sommerfeld for tea anyway." This was only partly true because she also had some things to discuss with her friend.

She'd just come from Morton House where she'd dropped by for a chat with the duchess about her plans. As expected, Lady Morton found them deliciously wicked and would, of course, attend the country house party. Needless to say, she was going to be complicit in any way possible, but her plans also hinged upon the cooperation of Lady Sommerfeld—the one whose words had inspired Juliette to form this plan in the first place.

The last piece of the puzzle was the stubborn Scotsman standing before her. Juliette needed Lady Sommerfeld's help to nudge him in the right direction and convince him to agree to attend the party. She hadn't planned on encountering him on her way to speak to the viscountess, however.

"I…assume you received your invitation then?"

"I did," he replied, his tone much more sober as he released her elbow and stepped back a more respectable distance. "And I thank you for it; however, I don't believe I should attend."

"Ah, but that doesn't mean you won't."

She thought she heard him curse under his breath. "What is it that you want from me?" he hissed low enough that no servants could hear them from another room.

"I believe I made that rather clear." She spoke slowly, as if to a small child. "And you already agreed."

"It was in poor judgment; I was caught in a moment of weakness." He reached up as if to run a rough hand through his hair, but stopped short. "I am a busy man with a profession. While my life may seem stable enough, everything I've built hinges upon my credibility and trustworthiness. Not only will it look terrible if I need to cancel my appointments while I'm away, but what do you think will happen if word gets out that I'm defiling pretty young ladies?"

"I never said anything about 'defiling', and I trust that you would never take anything too far or behave in a manner that was disrespectful of my wishes."

"And why do you have so much faith in me?"

"Because you have taken great pains to help me. And you've been nothing but respectful." Her cheeks warmed when he cocked a brow at her statement. *Well, when he wasn't kissing her senseless…*

Ian looked around to make sure they were still alone before he quickly ushered her into the nearest room with a warm, firm hand on her lower back. It turned out to be the small parlor where Lord and Lady Sommerfeld typically received callers. He felt so large standing so close to her. His broad shoulders and chest took up most of her field of vision, the heat from his body engulfed her; his nearness was making it difficult for her to think, to breathe. He inclined his head so their gazes met. The afternoon light afforded her a brilliant view of his eyes, the golden flecks in his irises, the darker ring surrounding the vibrant pools of color.

"Why me?" he asked, his voice barely above a croak.

"Because," she breathed, struggling to find words when he was this close. "Because there is something about you," she added honestly. His eyes searched her face as if in disbelief, but he said nothing. Each passing second made her less sure of herself. Perhaps he really was having serious second thoughts. "Don't you wish to follow through?"

"More than you know," he groaned, sending a chill of awareness from the top of her head to the tips of her toes. He heaved an aggravated sigh at odds with the statement he'd just uttered. "Let me make sure I understand you. You want me to take time away from my work…to attend a house party for a week…?"

Juliette nodded enthusiastically. "I know you may need to do some rearranging of appointments, but you're welcome to bring your research with you." His eyes widened. "I saw some of the papers. On your desk. In your office." She flushed a little, embarrassed that she'd just admitted to snooping. He sighed again, but this time it was much more resigned. She chose to take that as a good sign. "Perhaps I will get my Gaelic tutor after all." This earned her a smile and an indulgent shake of his head. He stepped closer and she couldn't breathe at all as her heart leaped into her throat. His hand cupped her cheek, his thumb stroking her lower lip.

"You are a very, very singular woman, Juliette."

She lifted one shoulder in an attempt at nonchalance. "I know. But I am also a woman who has had far too little fun up to this point in my life." His pupils dilated. "If you want to be my accomplice, you need only accept the invitation, Ian." His eyes slid closed as his name crossed her lips. She experienced a thrill at the realization that she did have power. It was heady, indeed. He pressed his forehead to hers and took a deep breath. They stayed in that moment for several heartbeats until he released her and stepped away.

There was a slight creak on the stairs. They'd left the door open and Juliette stepped out, followed by Ian. Lady Sommerfeld paused in her descent, her pale hand upon the polished banister. It appeared that the butler had notified her of Juliette's arrival and her friend had come to greet her.

Lady Sommerfeld's indigo eyes looked from Juliette to Ian and back again. She gave the two of them a smile, but it was clear she sensed the tension. The air was thick with it.

"If you'll excuse me," Ian inclined his head and retrieved his medical bag. "Good day, ladies." He showed himself out.

Only after the heavy door shut securely behind him, did Juliette look back up at her friend still frozen on the stairs.

"Well," Lady Sommerfeld began airly; "that was quite interesting."

"I've never seen Ian so worked up before," Lady Sommerfeld chuckled over the spread of tea and biscuits set between them. "He's normally such a calm, even man."

Juliette pulled her lips between her teeth, trying not to grin like a madwoman. To have confirmation that she shook the even-keeled physician was thrilling. She'd spent the last half an hour explaining to her friend all that had transpired, and all of her motivations behind planning this country house party. And all she hoped might come of it.

Juliette had worried about how Lady Sommerfeld might receive her plans, but she'd reminded herself how supportive she'd been in the beginning. And this conversation was only confirmation of that.

"I'm never quite sure whether he wants to throttle me or kiss me again."

"Again?" her friend's auburn brows flew up toward her hairline. "That is a good sign."

Juliette set down her teacup and saucer. "I hope you don't take this the wrong way, but it still baffles me why you're being so supportive of…this." Juliette's cheeks began to burn. "Why you're helping to push us together."

"Plainly? Ian has never done anything he hasn't wanted to do. I may help nudge him in the right direction, but I am by no means influencing his obvious interest in you. He also has far too little fun in his life."

The last words made Juliette's heart skip.

They sounded so similar to the words she'd recently spoken to Ian. Perhaps the two of them needed this more than she'd thought…

"Don't misinterpret my actions, though," Meredith continued; "I am by no means condoning complete ruination." The pointed look she shot Juliette made her cheeks warm. "I'm merely…being lenient in allowing a dalliance. You are both two consenting adults here. You know your minds. Besides, I've come to know you quite well over the past several years, and Ian, well, I've known him since I was a girl—I suppose it's closer to two decades at this point. My, but doesn't that make one feel rather old."

Juliet nearly laughed with a very unladylike snort but stopped just shy. If Lady Sommerfeld was anything, it surely wasn't "old." If anything, she felt more like a sister than a matron; to be honest; the same went for the Duchess of Morton. The three of them made quite the trio. Lady Sommerfeld, widowed at a young age after being married off to a man far older than she, only to marry the mysteriously injured Viscount Sommerfeld. Lady Morton, married and abandoned all within a day. And Juliette...the sheltered spinster sister of an earl who cared for her so very deeply that he inadvertently stifled every aspect of her life in the name of protection.

Well, no more.

Juliette had quite literally had a taste of desire and there was no turning back.

"Knowing both your personalities as I do, I believe you complement one another quite well. And every girl should experience a little love affair in her life."

Juliette hadn't had a mother in almost ten years and she'd always wondered what it might be like to have a sister. Currently, she imagined it would be a great deal like having Meredith—filled with all sorts of delightful trouble and mischief.

Chapter Nine

Juliette spent the next two weeks preparing their country house for the party. She had to coordinate shipping her necessities, but it was rather convenient to have a fair stock of things already in the country. The staff had to be notified to open and air out the rooms for guests. The stores had to be counted and restocked. She'd sketched out a general menu, but looked forward to meeting with their housekeeper and cook to finalize everything. She took great pains to plan outings and activities. There was still much to be done, but she tried to accomplish as much as she could from London. By the time Ethan was ready to leave, she was fairly bouncing in place in anticipation. Of course, she had to be particularly careful to temper her excitement, lest Ethan wonder why she was inordinately excited about a rather small, relaxed house party.

In addition to Ian, Lord and Lady Sommerfeld, and the Duchess of Morton, several of her brother's friends would also be attending. She'd balanced out their numbers by inviting a few eligible women from her reading society—friends who would be grateful for the opportunity to be out of London and enjoy the freedoms to be experienced in the country.

The day before they departed from London, Juliette received a note from Ian. The single line of slanted writing indicated he would do his best to attend if his schedule permitted it.

Then, a few hours later, a second delivery arrived…as if the sender had debated about forwarding it along to her. When she opened it up (safely away from her brother's prying eyes, just in case), she found a small, old book, well-worn and well-loved. It was barely bigger than her hand, with yellowed pages and a fragile brown fabric cover smudged with years of tiny fingerprints. She opened the cover to find a lilting language and plate line drawings illuminating the stories within.

It was a Gaelic book for children. A note fluttered out from between the pages and into her lap. It was a small scrap of parchment with only two words in the same sprawling, masculine script as earlier: *Start simple.*

Juliette smiled instantly, keenly aware of just how sweet a gesture the book was.

"Another book for your reading society?"

Juliette jumped, nearly dropping the book and the note to the floor as her brother strode into the parlor. She hadn't expected to see him again until supper, but there he was, carrying a thick book along with him.

She choked on her words and prayed he would accept her simple nod in response. She tucked it away against her hip, carefully disguising it beneath the folds of her skirt until she could slip away to her rooms and pack it safely away.

*****

Juliette was adjusting one last flower arrangement on the circular table in the entryway when the crunch of gravel and jangle of tack echoed up the long drive. The first of her guests were arriving, one by one, carriage by carriage. Lord and Lady Sommerfeld shared Lady Morton's carriage. A few of her brother's friends arrived on horseback, having sent their trunks ahead with their valets. One by one, they filtered inside, were greeted warmly, and shown to their rooms to freshen up after their journeys. As each one arrived, her anticipation only grew…until Ian's hired private coach finally pulled into the drive. She experienced a small pang of guilt because she knew such a thing did not come cheaply; however, she really couldn't have offered to send the Hopesend carriage back for him. Good lord, but what would Ethan have thought of that? Instead, Juliette chose to be honored that Ian had agreed to attend even though it was inconvenient for both his purse and his business.

She did her best to affect the calm, cool collection expected of a hostess, careful to wait the appropriate amount of time to greet Ian so he would not realize just how long she'd been shooting glances out the manor's many front windows for his arrival.

The subtle glitter in his eyes, however, told her he knew she'd done just that.

His trunks and boxes were carried in one after another by the footmen. It was immediately apparent that he had taken her offer to bring his work to the house party.

"He and my husband's brother share a similar penchant for packing 'light,'" murmured Lady Sommerfeld with a conspiratorial chuckle as Ian was led away, followed by the trail of luggage like ducklings. He'd been distant and composed upon greeting her, but Juliette feared her nerves and excitement were becoming too evident. He'd come, which meant he'd well and truly accepted her offer. And she couldn't wait to get started.

*****

That evening, there was a light, informal supper served for those who wished to eat with company rather than retire to their rooms. As luck would have it, Juliette was the only lady in attendance; Lady Sommerfeld had been exhausted from traveling and the viscount had opted to stay with her; Lady Morton had a headache because she never seemed to remember that she always developed one when she read while traveling in a coach; the rest of Juliette's friends had opted to stay in their rooms with their chaperones. This was, of course, not to say that Ethan's friends weren't perfectly polite to her, but it was exhausting being the only woman in attendance. It would normally have been considered inappropriate, but this was a relaxed country dinner and her brother's watchful eyes never left her. As was his custom, he'd smoothly interject if he felt one of them was too interested in her. He needn't have worried; the only thing more of a deterrent than a hawkeyed male relative would have been if she'd worn a dress made from angry bees.

Following dessert of berries and clotted cream atop a moist spongecake, the men excused themselves to chat over drinks and cigars in the library—of course, not until each one politely offered to refuse to leave her alone. She declined their offers gracefully, especially because she could tell they would all much rather enjoy whatever it was men discussed when they were outside of a female's delicate ears...

Rather than sit alone in the large parlor, she decided to retire for the evening. It didn't look as if much of anything exciting would happen that evening. The house was quiet. She could rest peacefully knowing she'd accomplished an uneventful start to the house party. Only...

Just the thought of Ian residing under the same roof as she made her pulse trip over itself like a gangly filly.

He hadn't joined them for supper. She wondered if he'd eaten alone and was just then lying atop the comfortable bed in the room she'd chosen for him. Was he a restless sleeper, as busy in repose as he was during the day? Or did he sleep like the dead to recuperate from his neverending schedule?

Juliette was wrenched from her wayward thoughts when she reached up to tuck a loose curl behind her ear and noticed she'd lost one of her earrings.

"Drat," she muttered. It must have been knocked loose during supper—the emerald earrings had been her grandmother's and tended to come loose. She was exactly halfway to her rooms at that point; she could have continued on and sent her maid back to look for it, but that seemed needless. It would take far less time for her to retrace her steps and check the spot where she'd sat during the meal. Resolved to handle it herself, she turned around and headed back to the first-floor landing only to collide with a solid wall of man as it came around a blind corner to the same landing.

Large, warm hands caught her upper arms to steady her. Juliette's breath caught harshly in her chest when she looked up into Ian's ruggedly handsome face. All rational thought fled her and her brain melted into slush. Those well-formed lips of his tilted into a hint of a smile.

"Headed down to supper?" he asked, casting a glance at the small clock on the landing's half-moon table. "I thought I'd missed it."

"You did," she started and then slowed her speech to sound a little less eager to be conversing with him. "I mean, yes. Supper was at half-seven."

"A shame." His thumbs stroked the skin between her cap sleeves and her long gloves once. Twice. Another time and she might just press herself against him there in plain view for anyone to see.

"A—Are you hungry? Let us find you something to eat." She didn't give him a chance to decline and latched onto a thread of boldness, taking his hand in hers and leading him back down the stairs to the ground floor.

"I wouldn't want to put you out." His tone was hesitant, but the way his fingers intertwined with hers was unexpectedly warm and lovely. They fit.

"Not at all! I was headed back down anyway. Lost my earring, you see." Juliette gestured to her naked earlobe and guided him toward the dining room after listening and confirming her brother and his friends were still occupied on the far side of the house. "We just need to make a quick detour to the dining room to find it, and then we can slip down to the kitchens to find you a bite."

Reluctantly, she slid her hand from Ian's as they entered the dining room. The efficient staff had begun cleaning as soon as she'd left the room and the footmen and maids froze in their tasks and greeted her with deference when she entered.

"Is there anything I can do for you, Lady Juliette?" inquired James, the under-butler.

"Thank you, no," she replied with a smile. "I've just come to find —my earring!" She snapped up the glittering bauble from beneath the chair she'd sat in during the meal. Holding it aloft, she grinned triumphantly and affixed it to her ear. "There." She turned back to Ian and tilted her chin to indicate they should leave through the door from which they'd entered. She led him back up the hallway, past the stairs, to a disguised doorway cleverly papered over to match the wall. "They'll make a fuss if we ask them for food for you," she explained. "It's easier and quicker if we just do it ourselves. They've all worked so hard to ready the house and I'd rather not cause a stir this late in the evening." She pressed open the servants' doorway to the close flight of stairs used by the staff to traverse the full height of the house, from the basement kitchens to their private quarters on the topmost floor of the manor. A glance over her shoulder provided an amusing scene. The width of Ian's shoulders made the narrow staircase seem even more so; indeed, he looked far too big to be attempting this route. The corners of his mouth were turned down in concentration.

"This seems like a great deal of trouble—"

"Not at all!"

He made a grunt of disbelief before his large hand cupped her elbow from behind to steady her as they turned on the landing. His skin was so warm, his palm slightly roughened from his work.

She stopped when they reached the lowest floor; Ian halted as closely behind her as they could without touching her. She could feel his heat along the length of her back and she had to fight the nearly overwhelming urge to lean back into him.

Instead, she glanced at Ian over her shoulder, pressing her finger to her lips to signal that he should remain silent and wait for her. She turned the corner into the golden light pouring out from the kitchens.

She'd always loved sneaking down here as a girl—before her health had forbidden such adventures, and then her parents' cautiousness prevented it even after she'd recovered. It was always warm and smelled of citrus and herbs, woodsmoke and flour. The long plank table was worn satin-smooth from decades of being scrubbed clean with sand. The happy chatter floated on the steamy air as the cookmaids and scullery maids tidied and scrubbed pots and dishes. One footman lingered in the corner out of earshot of the rest as he and an upstairs maid whispered with inclined heads—a clear courtship if ever there was one. Juliette might have mentioned something to young Hattie about being careful, but, for one, who was Juliette to say anything about just such a situation? Ian was mere feet away waiting for her. And she knew Francis was a good lad from a lovely family who would rather harm himself than another person. Hattie could do far worse than he.

"Lady Juliette!" Cookie caught sight of her as she stepped from the larder and back into the bustling kitchen. The ensuing expectant silence and eyes upon her made Juliette want to squirm like a child. "What can we do for you?"

"Oh, don't mind me!" she waved her hands and giggled uncomfortably. "Go about your business. I'm just here to filch some leftovers."

"Was supper not to your liking?"

"Oh, no! It was lovely!" she rushed to reassure the cook who'd been in her family's employ since before Juliette's birth. She wished she'd formulated a good excuse on the way down to the kitchens, but it had been so intoxicating being alone with Ian that no other thoughts had been allowed into her brain. She couldn't very well say she was personally retrieving food for him—that would no doubt get back to her brother, whether accidentally or with good intentions—so she fumbled for something else. "I know Lady Sommerfeld didn't have a chance to try your delicious supper, so I thought I would take a plate to her when I look in on my way to my rooms."

Juliette realized her mistake as soon as the words left her lips and a frown passed over Cookie's plump features. Of course, Lord and Lady Sommerfeld had had trays sent up while they rested. She'd never been brilliant at thinking on the fly when there were at least half a dozen pairs of eyes watching her.

"Well," the cook said finally, wiping her hands on her apron. "Why don't we just gather up some things…" It was obvious that the older woman didn't believe Juliette, but she also didn't seem to be able to parse out the truth. This served Juliette just fine as she supervised the heaping of a plate with rolls and thick slices of cold beef roast crusted in herbs from the kitchen gardens. Juliette added a cluster of fat grapes beside the remaining slice of sponge cake and berries and accepted the plate from the cook.

"You have Lady Sommerfeld let us know when she's finished. You keep fetching and serving the guests, then His Lordship will have our heads for not doing our duties."

"Of course, Cookie. Thank you again."

Juliette found Ian standing still and silent as a sentinel in the dim stairwell. She tilted her chin toward the stairs and he took the plate from her before allowing her to lead the way.

They reached the first floor and slipped into the dimly lit hallway. Juliette had one more floor to climb before she reached the family bedchambers, but there was no sense in continuing to use the servants' stairwell.

"Thank you. For this," Ian said, holding up the plate piled high with food.

"Of course." She offered him a smile, suddenly much shier than she had been when she'd concocted this scheme of hers. She cleared her throat as daintily as possible. "I'll leave you to it, then. Have a lovely evening and I will see you—" Ian's hand upon her arm stopped her words and her body from retreating.

"I eat alone so often, I would be quite glad of the company. That is if you are not overtired from today."

"Not at all!" she replied far too swiftly for any sort of dignity. If Ian minded, then his small grin did well to hide it. "Come with me." She proceeded to lead him up one additional flight of stairs to the family floor. In addition to the family bedchambers and private sitting rooms, there was also a lovely glass-paned gazebo. It was quite unique in its design and construction, being on the topmost floor of the wing with large Easterly-facing windows on three sides. It made one feel as if she sat on top of the world. It had always been one of Juliette's favorite places, even when she was a little girl clinging to her mother's skirts.

Ethan hadn't entered the room since their parents' passing; still, Juliette had diligently requested that the room always be tidied and aired whenever they were in residence. It was her escape. And it was also the safest place for her to spend uninterrupted time with Ian because she was entirely confident her brother would never interrupt.

She plucked a candle from a sconce in the hallway and carried it along. Ian moved surprisingly silently for a man of his size as he trailed closely behind her. Together, they ducked into the room and she pressed the heavy door closed before flitting about and lighting several candles placed around the room. She could have lit more, but too much glow would ruin the effect of the velvet night and diamond stars outside the expansive windows.

She turned to find that Ian had set his plate of food on a table set between a pair of spindle chairs and was staring out into the night. The fine fabric of his coat was stretched taut across his broad shoulders as he crossed his arms over his chest.

"Quite the view," he whispered, catching the reflection of her movement in the glass when she came up beside him.

"It is, isn't it? I always loved coming up here as a child." They smiled at one another. "You needn't whisper. No one will be able to hear us," she added. His eyes lowered to her lips and her cheeks warmed when she realized just how her words could be interpreted.

The way his dark gaze caressed her mouth told her he may very well have interpreted those words just so. Her heart kicked up a more frantic beat; her breath became stuck in her throat and made her suddenly lightheaded.

She'd been nearly silly with anticipation of finding herself alone with Ian once again and, now that she was quite literally confronted with the moment, she found herself nervous all over again. What she wouldn't have given for an ounce of the confidence she'd felt when she'd concocted the scheme and coerced him into attending this house party.

His large hand lifted ever so slowly until one of his fingers trailed across her cheek softly enough that she might have imagined it. That blunt fingertip seared a path up the curve of her cheek to gently re-place a lock of her hair behind her ear and it lingered there.

He seemed as indecisive as she.

Ian had only to slide his fingers into her hair and tug her to him; she knew she would gladly fall into his arms if he did so. She'd sur-render herself to his whims and, together, they would fan the flames of the desire that had simmered between them since the moment he'd come to her rescue all those weeks ago.

Instead, Ian's hand dropped, a rueful tilt to his lips, and he turned back to the small table behind them.

"Will you join me?" he asked, pulling out one of the chairs for her.

She could only nod and soon the two of them were sitting together at the table, so close that his long legs brushed her skirts, his knee pressed into hers and she did not pull away. She savored the heat and hardness of it.

Chapter Ten

Likewise, Ian was far from unmoved by Juliette's nearness. Despite his most concerted efforts, he'd pondered little else in the days leading up to his trip to the countryside; each passing mile of that journey served only to inflame his anxious desire to be with her once more. He wanted to hear her voice, watch the way her dimples deepened when she smiled, bathe in her intoxicating scent, feel the softness of her skin and her lips beneath his. Perhaps most perplexing was his near-desperate need to simply talk with her. He longed to know what she thought of the book he'd sent to her. He wanted to know what else she was reading for her Society. And what else amused her and made her smile.

And now that the time had come, he was embarrassed about how nervous he was.

He was no lad, but a man solidly in his third decade of life. He wasn't inexperienced by any means or any sense of the word. He was confident in his abilities and his knowledge. But there was something about being there with Juliette within arm's reach that set him on his ear. She made the world tilt and turned his insides to mush. It only served to amplify his mild discomfort about eating in front of her—if his mother had done anything, it was to instill proper manners in him until they were as natural as breathing.

This dissipated like mist when Juliette leaned forward and plucked a few plump grapes from the pile upon his plate, smiling as she popped one into her mouth. Little did she know, the innocuous action made his insides melt even more.

There was something incredibly intimate about the small gesture; something surprisingly comfortable. His mind turned it over and over as his mouth enjoyed the savory meal the Hopesend kitchen staff had prepared.

"You could have sent for a servant to bring you supper, you know. We are fully staffed for the party."

Ian finished chewing before responding. "I'm not all that comfortable requesting something so simple be done for me, not when I'm fully capable." He proceeded to cut another piece of roast meat. "I don't employ a valet either; it's why I dress so simply because I need to be able to do it myself. Mrs. Brown—the woman you met when you stopped by my offices—is the extent of my hired help. She handles the cooking and cleaning."

"Ah," Juliette replied, her eyes glittering. "So there is no one to care for you besides your rather formidable gatekeeper." The words were far from unkind, perhaps even somewhat admirable toward the older woman's tenacity. "May I ask why it makes you so uncomfortable to have others wait on you?"

He lifted a shoulder. "As you may have suspected, I did not grow up with servants." He hesitated, unsure how much of his life and past to divulge, but the earnest glint in her fathomless eyes, the way she leaned toward him as he spoke, decided for him. "My mother worked as a maid in a household in Edinburough to help fund my education and provide support as I moved on to medical school. I witnessed firsthand how hard she worked to earn what little she could; it was disproportionate. Even though I earned a scholarship, there were still everyday expenses and other necessities to cover. The courses were so rigorous they left little time to sleep, let alone hold a job to pay for us both." He skimmed over the part where he'd always been forced to work twice as hard to earn half the accolades as his English class-mates, or those with enough money to afford schooling without schol-arship. Sensing a kindred soul, Meredith's uncle had seen his potential and, in addition to mentoring him, he'd offered Ian a paid apprentice-ship. Ian's mother had never once complained about the sacrifices she'd made to support him, which made it all the sweeter when he'd been able to pay the rent on their small flat for the very first time.

Juliette seemed to think on his words very carefully, perhaps con-sidering what it might have been like to grow up less fortunate, as she fiddled with a fold in her skirt. "And your father?" she inquired.

Ian set down his fork as a knife of ice struck him in the sternum. Words would not come at first.

"You needn't answer if you do not wish to." Ian's eyes flew to Juliette's face when she spoke. The calm warmth there was comfort-ing and welcoming in an unfamiliar way, but Ian was grateful for it. The tension immediately melted from his body and, suddenly, the words fell from his lips.

"He died. When I was a lad." The sting of it was still raw as a blis-ter, even after all these years.

Juliette's small, pale hand covered his. "I'm sorry," she whispered, absorbing the poignant grief in his tone. They shared a moment of comradery only those who've lost parents too early can comprehend. Ian turned his palm up and allowed her to weave her fingers with his.

"I was born and bred in the Highlands, like many of my family's generations before me. The land is beautiful and wild; the people are just as rugged and hardy, singular in their determination to preserve the old ways of life. Unfortunately, the remoteness of the lifestyle means proper medical care can be few and far between, and what little there is, is of poor quality. More than half of it is antiquated, consisting of superstitions and treatments that do nothing.

"My father fell ill when I was younger." Ian paused, focusing on the feel of Juliette's fragile fingers on his own, his thumb stroking the cup of her palm. A wistful smile danced across his lips. "I remember him as a big bear of a man with the largest hands I've ever seen. He had a laugh like thunder and a heart of gold... Toward the end, he was gray and frail." The image still haunted Ian. He'd ached with helplessness as he'd been forced to watch the man he worshiped and admired waste away into nothingness; as he witnessed every breath become a gasping labor when his lungs weren't consumed with fits of violent coughing. "Many people in our village died from the same illness. Young and old were the first, then even the hale and hardy succumbed. The sickness didn't discriminate. I still believe with every fiber of my being that something could have been done—some of them could have been saved—if there had only been proper medical care available to us."

Juliette was silent.

Ian looked up to find her examining him, her eyes suspiciously bright.

"This is why you became a physician," she murmured. He nodded once in reply and released her hand to resume eating to mask the

swell of emotion ebbing through his chest. He did his best not to focus too much on the loss of Juliette's warmth.

She remained quiet for several minutes. He could feel the caress of
her eyes upon him, as tangible as a lover beside him in bed. She made
his skin tingle and his blood heat several degrees until he felt as if he
was boiling from the inside out.

He hadn't believed his good fortune when he'd bumped into her on
the stairs. It had taken all of his self-control to not seek her out earlier,
but some benevolent deity must have found him worthy of grace because he had found her when he'd least expected to. Every one of his
senses had been on fire since that moment of collision.

The night had been growing only better with each ill-advised decision—when he'd followed her down the servants' stairs to the
kitchens and allowed her to scrounge up supper for him; when, for
some reason, he'd asked her to keep him company while he ate; when
he'd followed her up to this remote corner of the manor; and, now,
when they sat alone together in the dim room, the stars winking at
them through the tall glass windows, making everything seem more
intimate and expansive at the same time.

She looked stunning sitting there beside him in half-golden candlelight and half-mysterious shadow. Her cream-colored lace gown was
elegant in its understated finery, highlighting her luminous skin with
its hint of golden glow. He noticed, when they'd been pressed close
together in the servants' stairwell, that she smelled faintly of roses and
warm skin, something uniquely Juliette, delicate and enticing. A scent
that made him ache with need, his sex unbearably heavy in his
breeches.

The entire carriage ride, Ian had been consumed with questioning
his sanity. The days since Juliette had stopped by his office had been
nothing but spinning in mental circles as he contemplated the voracity

of his morals and decisions. And, yet, still, he found himself beneath the roof belonging to the very powerful brother of the woman who had taken over both his conscious and unconscious thoughts. It was ill-advised, to say the least. Reckless and unconscionable, to be honest. But, seated there in the intimate lighting, their legs brushing beneath the table, Ian had never felt anything so right.

His appetite having shifted, Ian set aside his silverware and shoved his chair back from the table. He held out his hand to Juliette, his pulse pounding through his body to a deafening degree.

"Come here," he rasped. Her beautiful eyes bounced from his face to his hand and then back before she placed her fingers in his and stood.

All rational thought lost, Ian tugged her into his lap and marveled at how well they fit together.

"Ian," she breathed, her cheeks catching fire.

"Where has the brazen lass gone?" he murmured and wrapped his arms around her slim frame. She had the most delectable shape; he could tell the curves of her bottom were pure perfection even through the damnable layers of clothing between them. A rush of fire filled his abdomen, dripping lower with molten need. She squeaked when he pressed his lips to the pulse in her throat and inhaled deeply.

"I—I...that is—oh!" Her words died abruptly when he nibbled the lobe of her ear, right behind the earring that had so helpfully come loose earlier and allowed them to find one another.

His hands caressed her back, cupped her hip, traced the delectable curve of her waist, ached to test the weight of her breast with his palm or dip to that warm, forbidden hollow between her legs.

Juliette's hands were performing a tentative exploration of their own. Gooseflesh prickled every inch of his skin when she flattened her palm against his chest, and then slid upward to the edge of his cravat, curling around the back of his neck. Her fingers tangled in the strands at the nape of his neck, holding him close as he tasted the sensitive skin of her jaw.

"You still want this?" he murmured against her skin.

"Hmm?" Her head tilted back as he nuzzled her throat.

His hands tightened around her until their bodies were entirely flush with one another. "This," he growled. "Me."

Her breathing hitched and her body stilled. He loosened his grip enough to allow her to lean back a few inches to look into his face.

"Are you asking me if I've changed my mind?"

Ian's jaw clenched by way of a reply. He didn't want to know the answer, but he had to. It had been the only other thought occupying his mind for the past several days. He knew he would release her immediately if she'd come to her senses and decided to call off whatever harebrained scheme she'd concocted.

He could see her pulse flickering in her throat.

"I haven't," she finally whispered.

It was all the urging Ian needed to pull her head down to his, capturing her lips, claiming her mouth with his own. The faint whimper escaping from her throat caused a scarlet haze to burst behind his eyes and surge throughout his body. His grip must have been nearly painful on her waist and the back of her neck, but she only clutched him closer. Both of them were panting when he finally broke the kiss.

"If I ever do something you do not desire," he forced out the words through lips which seemed to have lost the power of speech; "if ever there is something you do not wish, you need only tell me and I will listen. Say a word and I will stop."

She gazed down at him, her pupils so dilated they nearly engulfed the color of the irises. "You can't ever do something I don't wish you to do." Her voice was slightly tremulous but clear and honest.

"Good," Ian growled. "Because I've thought of little else beyond this—" he squeezed her against him—"in days." He craned his neck to capture her lips once again, a low moan eked unbidden from his chest when she met him with equal fervor. Her palms slid up the curve of his chest to grip his shoulders. What he wouldn't give to have her straddling him, his straining cock nestled in the sweet heat at the crux of her thighs.

But Ian's lust-hazed mind still knew there had to be a line he did not cross. They must not do anything irrevocable, no matter how they might crave it. The onus was on him as the more experienced of them to maintain restraint and a reasonable hold upon his sanity…though Lord knew it would be one of the most difficult ventures of his life. He was ravenous for this woman.

Their lips met in a frenzy, the click of teeth and breathless sighs filled the air of their little golden-lit bubble. It was easy to believe the rest of the world outside of this intimate space had melted away, evaporated with the heat of whatever it was that had burned so brightly between them from the very first. Having Juliette in his arms felt right, even though every fiber of his being screamed that it was so, so wrong. So dangerous. In more ways than one.

She pressed herself more closely to him, unconsciously rocking her hips against him in an instinctive rhythm. Ian's breath hissed through his teeth. Even if Juliette was untried and innocent there remained, buried deep within her, primal urges. The femininity in her body knew the masculinity in his; it knew what to do, knew what it craved as naturally as how to keep her heart beating and her breath moving in and out of her lungs.

"Tell me what you want," he growled against her mouth. She whimpered in response, shaking her head, unable to voice what she desired. "This?" he demanded, his large palms cupping the perfectly rounded globes of her bottom in a bruising grip. "You want my hands on you, lass?" His voice was growing harsher, the Scottish burr coming through more thickly with each second of the delectable torture of having Juliette in his arms, but not naked beneath him. "What are your plans with me?"

"This," Juliette hissed, her fingers twining through his hair almost painfully, her teeth scraping his lower lip. "More of this."

Ian growled, happy—nay, eager—to oblige. He shoved his half-eaten supper across the table to create just enough space for what he intended. Rocking his weight forward, he stood enough to slide Juliette's bottom on the tabletop and propped her there. He pressed closer, nestling himself between her legs, standing over her, dominating her with his size, never breaking contact with his lips and tongue. She had to angle her head back to accommodate his height. Her hands, no longer able to reach his head, slipped down to his waistcoat to fist in the fitted silk. She was likely to leave wrinkles, but Ian didn't care one whit. In fact, he knew he'd smile fondly upon those creases later when he saw them and recalled this interlude.

Juliette's head fell back on a sigh when his lips trailed down her jaw.

"There are more places a man can kiss a woman to give her pleasure."

"Oh?" she sighed, somewhat belatedly.

"Aye," Ian breathed harshly. "Here." He pressed his open mouth to the spot where her jaw met her neck.

"Here." He nipped her earlobe and then soothed it with a kiss.

"Here." He tasted the pounding pulse in her throat.

"Here…" He kissed the milky expanse of her decolletage exposed above the edge of her gown. He was enveloped in her intoxicating scent.

What he wouldn't give to bury his face just there.

He teetered on a dangerous precipice of his self-control. He was mere inches away from all loss of sanity. He'd thought of little else but this woman in his arms; knowing her mind had been similarly tortured was heady. It drove him wild. It awoke something barbaric and untamed within him. It roared to life within him like a blistering mountain wind through heather. It made him tighten his grip on Juliette's body, tangle his fingers in her hair, and yank her mouth to his once more to plunder her with his tongue. It bellowed at him to tear off her clothes and devour her.

The last thought was like a bucket of icy water over his head and Ian wrenched himself away from Juliette as if he'd been scorched. His chest heaved in time with the rise and fall of Juliette's delectable bosom. He had to be the one in charge of drawing a line in this wildly absurd situation. The onus was on him to maintain restraint. It might kill him, but he knew what he must do.

Juliette's heavily lidded eyes met his. He knew his pupils were likely as ravenous as hers were. Ian removed his shaking hand from her rear and tucked a loose black curl of hair behind her ear. Those mesmerizing eyes of hers slid closed and she tilted her head into his touch. It took everything he had not to send his senses to hell and take her right then and there.

"I fear we may have underestimated our chemistry." Ian's chuckle was as weak as his voice. "Might I suggest we part ways for the evening?" He cut off her mewl of protest by gently pressing his thumb to her lips. He couldn't resist tracing the plump pillow of her lower lip with the pad of his thumb. It was a mistake, however, because he was nearly undone all over again when those lips parted, gifting him with a little glimpse of her pearly teeth and carnation-pink tongue. He cleared his throat, but his voice was still noticeably husky. "This is not to say you haven't considered everything and the implications therein, but I think we would be wise to keep our wits about us. And you must think on what exactly you hope to get out of this rather dangerous plan of yours."

"Dangerous?" she laughed incredulously. She wouldn't ask that if she knew exactly where his mind went… Ian didn't dignify the question with a straightforward response; he was too afraid he would describe, in vivid detail, all the things he wanted to do to her.

"Now that this…is out of our system, I need you to think clearly about what you want."

"What I want?" She leaned back a little, her shapely brows knitting together. "I told you want I want—"

"I know what you desire," he said, cutting her off, doing everything in his power not to grind upwards and make his meaning blatant. "What do you *want*? Where should the line be drawn? Because you and I both know there is no permanence here." At least, they did when their minds and bodies weren't otherwise occupied. He watched as Juliette's eyes fluttered down, shielding her gaze beneath the fan of her impossibly long coal-colored lashes.

"Stolen kisses in the dark? A few forbidden caresses? A little taste of pleasure?" Her cheeks flared as he said the last, but her eyes did not return to his face. "I can give you those." He crooked a finger beneath her chin, forcing her to look back at him. "I will *gladly* give you those, Juliette." Her blush deepened, but the desire in her eyes was unmistakable, bold.

Ian knew he needed to get away from Juliette before any more of his faculties fled him…before he did anything both of them would regret.

"It's important that you are certain about what you want to happen between us. The last thing I want is for this to end poorly. For you to regret anything." She opened her mouth to speak, but closed her lips once more, seeming to think better of what she'd been about to say. "The last thing I want is you to be hurt."

"And you?" she whispered. "What about you?"

"Me?" Ian barely stifled an incredulous chuckle.

"You have feelings as well, do you not?" she clarified with a charmingly innocent tilt of her head. Lord, if only she knew how many feelings he had. The realization that she was concerned about him in this situation was sobering and heady at the same time; it both thrilled him and made him nervous.

"You need not worry about me." His voice was husky, rich with everything pounding through his veins.

"And why not?" She wrinkled her nose most charmingly, an expression that would have sent many a Society matron into a fit of vapors. Whether she realized it or not, her fingers tangled in the hair at the nape of his neck, twisting and twining in a way that began to drive him mad with need. If they weren't careful, then they would wind up tangled in one another again. "You may be a man, but I would think you would have…opinions about all of this. In fact, I would wager you have more opinions than I do because you're so obviously more experienced."

This time, Ian did release a bark of laughter. His hands tightened around her. "You would be incredibly accurate in that assessment; I do have a great deal more fodder for my imagination. But, while I do appreciate your concern, you needn't worry. Truly." He added the last when she lifted a disbelieving brow. And then he sobered because he needed her to understand how treacherous this situation was. It wasn't that he didn't believe she knew her mind or was blind to the dangers, but this was more than a stolen peck on the lips from a titled lordling at a ball. Ian was of a different class, a different world than she. And he had accepted an illicit invitation right beneath an earl's nose. "Kisses, I will gladly give—a fact I believe I have made abundantly clear at this point. Holding you, touching you, are all things on the table. But how far do you wish this to go, Juliette? Where is the line you have drawn in that brilliant mind of yours?"

She chewed her lower lip and lowered her eyes, tilting her head away from him. They sat there in that compromising position for several minutes of silence. It should have been awkward and uncomfortable, but it wasn't. Ian wanted to give Juliette all the time she needed to mull over her reply. When she finally did speak, she did so to the ceiling, to the walls, the cavernous, glass-filled room around them.

"This used to be my mother's favorite room in the manor. Here, she would read, sew, and enjoy the view of the lands. It was always such a treat to be invited here into this sanctuary." Her luminous eyes met his. "I spent a great deal more time here with her when I became ill." Ian's heart stuttered. "Scarlet Fever struck when I was seven years of age. My brother remained well—he, as the heir, was moved to another house under an abundance of caution as soon as the illness began to spread. I survived, just barely, but many children in the village did not. As if the weeks of fevers and hallucinations weren't enough, I was sapped of all my vitality, my strength, my joy… My mother would bundle me up in a nest of quilts on that sofa. She would read to me, coax me into sipping barley water and bone broth, and we would watch the clouds race one another across the sky. I don't remember being sick, but I remember recovering. I remember her. My health was so precarious that it caused everyone to treat me with kid gloves from then on. Even after my stamina grew and I was no longer piqued by a walk to the gardens, I was not allowed to do anything for myself. Everyone lived in constant fear that that outing, that exertion, that trip and fall so common in every childhood would, inexplicably, be the one to deplete me and do me in.

"I was not allowed to join my brother's riding lessons. I couldn't walk to the village or climb trees anymore. Anything above carrying two books to my rooms was considered too strenuous and, therefore, strictly forbidden. I was never even allowed to learn how to dance." Pain flickered across her vision. Though Ian ached to comfort her, he could tell there was more she wished to say. He remained dutifully still as he listened. "The pattern continued after our parents were killed in a carriage accident and my brother became the new Earl of Hopesend...but it was different. Ethan survived my illness with his own trauma. He is my twin and we have always been closer than most siblings. When he thought he was going to lose me, it was not just the loss of a sibling he feared, but the horrible notion that he would be losing a part of himself. As such, he has developed a different sense of what is 'right' for me, and what is 'safe.' So, I attend my Reading Society meetings, I have few friends, and I do not attend balls where I would risk becoming overheated in a crush or—heaven forbid—asked to dance! Men do not court me, I suspect nearly as much for the fact that I am so secluded as the reality of just who my brother is. Everyone fears crossing him, so they do as he says. I am guarded like a precious porcelain doll. But with you, Ian...with you I feel like a woman for the first time in my life."

This, Ian understood.

It wasn't all that uncommon in families who had both suffered tragedy or narrowly escaped a tragic end. The reaction was often a way for them to hold onto what they had left and guard it with everything they had—whether or not those efforts were entirely rational. This, it would seem, would be exactly what the earl had been doing with Juliette. This vibrant woman had been condemned to a half-life because of her brother's fear of losing her. And, in doing so, he had pushed her into Ian's arms.

While it was tragic and Ian certainly felt sorry for Juliette, he couldn't be too broken up about it. It had, after all, brought her to him —brought them to this very moment—however brief a time that may be.

Still, ever a physician, Ian asked, "And you have no lasting I'll effects? No fluttering of your heart, dizzy spells, or periods of difficult breathing?"

"Not you, too," Juliette groaned and made to push off of Ian's chest; however, his hands held fast.

"I wouldn't be who I am If I didn't show care for your physical well-being."

"And what about my mental well-being?" she demanded. "I have never felt more myself than when you look at me; when you touch me, Ian. I don't believe etiquette lessons quite cover the proper way to admit such a thing to a man, so here I am treading into entirely uncharted waters and I hope it does not put you off of whatever this is." She gestured to the limited space between them. "But I would not have you think you are in any way taking advantage of me. If anything, it is I who is taking advantage of you."

She truly believed she was the one taking advantage here? Ian was practically struck dumb by the admission. He wanted to tell her she was wrong—that she was the epitome of delicate, well-bred fragility and he should have been drawn and quartered for even a fraction of the filthy things he'd imagined doing to her in the days since they had first met—but her earlier statements told him that would be precisely the wrong thing to say. The last thing Juliette wanted was to be viewed as the weak invalid she'd been treated as for so many years. That very view had deprived her of so many experiences and, while

Ian had little to nothing to offer her, he could give her this much. He would offer her a taste of desire and passion here at this house party. It was an impermanent arrangement, but he would give her everything he could.

"So," Juliette continued; "I will take what you are willing to share. Be it your Gaelic to assuage my thirst for languages, your time…or something else. Because it is all foreign and new and exciting. And I will cherish it."

Ian gently tugged her closer and pressed his lips to her forehead.

"I understand," he murmured against her soft skin. "For now, the hour grows late and we should both be off to our beds."

"There is an excursion and a picnic scheduled for tomorrow along with games. You will join us, won't you?"

"What sort of houseguest would I be if I didn't?"

"You did miss supper tonight." She shoved playfully at his shoulder.

"I consider this a working holiday; some of us do need to work for our livings." It was meant as a lighthearted jest, but the flicker in her eyes told him she hadn't considered such a thing and was torn between embarrassment and shame over her privileged lifestyle. He rushed to reassure her, saying, "Or I wasn't entirely sure how I was going to comport myself professionally when all I have been able to think about was pulling the beguiling hostess into my arms and kissing her senseless." None of it was a lie; not one bit.

It was also the right thing to say. Juliette's porcelain skin blushed prettily, temptingly. Ian placed one final peck upon the pert little tip of her nose and set her on her feet.

"Sleep on it," he murmured, standing so he once more towered over her. "I will see you tomorrow for the outing."

He was mesmerized by the way she pulled her full lower lip between her teeth as she nodded. He wondered if she was trying to find a taste of him there. Ian had to avert his gaze and clear his throat lest his body grow too excited.

"I will bid you good evening, then," she whispered, her words lost in the close shadows around them. She leaned forward and pressed a tender kiss to his cheek. "Thank you for coming. I—I am looking forward to the coming days," she breathed against his skin.

"*Oidhche mhath,*" he said. *Goodnight.*

Chapter Eleven

"Whoever did you bribe to obtain such glorious weather?" Lady Sommerfeld caught up with Juliette and hooked their arms together. She adjusted the ribbon on her bonnet as the breeze tugged at her playfully. It was a beautiful day—clear, sunny, and warm, though not overly so. Despite this, Ethan had threatened to cancel the outing when he discovered she had planned a walk to the folly by the fishing pond, but there was some deity smiling upon every aspect of that day because he had caved to pressure when it became clear that all their guests wished to partake in the outing. Ethan had bowed to Juliette's plans with the strict stipulation that she rest when needed and not overtax herself on the excursion. She had bitten her tongue and agreed to his overcautious demands.

The folly was a delightful little building in the form of a rectangular Grecian temple complete with Corinthian columns and replica statues of well-known masterpieces. It was charming in its absurd opulence and provided a lovely point at which to aim a walk. It glittered in winter and provided the perfect amount of shade on warm days. She had spent many a day reading and daydreaming at the small building, watching the clouds drift by and wishing she had been blessed with a healthier childhood and the freedom it afforded.

The folly had been erected by their grandfather beside the man-made fishing pond kept stocked with perch, pike, and other game fish —likely the main draw for the majority of the male guests. And, as Juliette was reminded when she shielded her eyes to look back at the rest of their party, it was only a few minutes' walk from the main house… She could still make out each window on the three-story building with its horseshoe-shaped layout and honey-colored stone. No matter how much she explained to Ethan that she'd (secretly) gone on longer walks through Hyde Park, told him she felt strong and healthy and there were no problems with her stamina, it mattered not to him. She was adamant that her brother needn't worry about her overdoing it on this short of a walk. In fact, she had planned it this way in the hopes that he would not object, but, alas, he maintained his poor estimation of her health. She'd been grateful for the pressure of their guests to help push through her plan.

The warm sunlight caught upon a glint of chestnut, dragging Juliette's eye back from the manor house. Many of the guests had been paired off in polite duos of men and women, but smaller groups had formed as the walk continued. Ethan, escorting the Duchess of Morton, had been joined by Lord Sommerfeld and the group adjusted their pace to accommodate the viscount's limping gait. Juliette had been originally escorted by her brother's friend, the affable Earl of Leighton; however, the man had excused himself to put his knowledge of entomology to good use and help identify a type of butterfly particularly enamored with the fresh flowers affixed to Baroness Pole's bonnet and reassure the poor, excitable woman that it was not, in fact, poisonous. Ian had the honor of escorting both Miss Jocelyn Finchley and her mother, as Mr. Finchley had declined to attend the outing. Ian listened kindly, intently, as Miss Finchley spoke, his chestnut head tilted in her direction. They ambled along, one woman on each arm, and it was difficult for Juliette not to stare…not to remember the way he had held her in those arms and touched her with those large hands. He seemed so much tamer in the daylight, so much less dangerous. But her skin tingled with the memories of the latent power he held in check. How could any woman be near him and not sense it?

"Stare any more intently and even flighty Lord Leighton will take note," Lady Sommerfeld muttered to Juliette beneath her breath, effectively tearing Juliette's eyes away from Ian.

"I have no antennae or mandibles, so I sincerely doubt that," Juliette retorted.

"For what it's worth," the red-haired woman leaned in conspiratorially; "he keeps sneaking glances at you, too." Both knew she wasn't referring to Lord Leighton.

Juliette ducked her head, hoping the brim of her bonnet would help disguise her growing flush. She was saved from having to reply as their party arrived at the folly. The surface of the pond was like glass, reflecting the glinting white stone of the folly set against the blue sky as a perfect mirror image. Servants had been sent ahead to lay out the blankets and overstuffed pillows, the wicker baskets of food and drink. Small bundles of wildflowers had been gathered and decorated each of the settings. Juliette surveyed the spread, pleased that she'd opted for a more casual arrangement where they sat on the thick green grass rather than asking for tables and chairs to be carted out from the manor. It seemed so frivolous when Mother Nature had already created such a glorious tableau.

"Are we placing wagers on biggest catch?" one of the men called out to Ethan. He wandered over to where the plethora of fishing tackle had been laid out for their pleasure.

"I hardly believe that is fair," her brother said as he guided Lady Morton to a cushion in the cool shade of the folly. "I've been fishing this pond since I was old enough to hold a pole."

"I'll take the bet," another man chimed in.

"Why not?" Lord Sommerfeld said with a shrug. Meredith smiled at her husband.

"Will you join us, Dr. McCullom?" the first man enquired as Ian approached with his walking partners.

"For?"

"A bit of fishing and a friendly wager," replied the second in an amiable tone.

"Thank you, no. I've never been one for fishing."

"I thought all Scots were avid outdoorsmen," Ethan said flippantly.

Juliette bit the inside of her cheek. Though Ian's smile remained unwavering, it did not meet his eyes. She thought she may have been the only one to notice the tautness around his mouth.

"I must have spent too much time in London and cities on the Continent for more rural pursuits," he finally said evenly.

"What do you do for fun, Dr. McCullom?" Mrs. Finchley asked innocently, oblivious to the low-grade tension.

"I find my medical practice does not allow for all that much time for pursuits of pleasure."

Juliette barely suppressed a shiver as the word "pleasure" crossed his lips.

"And no wife? No family?" harrumphed the older woman, much to her daughter's mortification. Any woman of marriageable age knew where this conversation was headed. "Such a shame that a man as intelligent, handsome, and respected as you remains *unmarried*. A crime, I say!"

Ian smiled indulgently as he helped her to her seat. "Alas, the opportunity has not presented itself."

Juliette was failing miserably at both not eavesdropping and remaining subtle about it.

"I find that difficult to believe!" the matron said dramatically, batting her eyes up at Ian. "Surely there are many women who would jump at the chance and even improve your life. A woman of a respectable family." Miss Finchley rolled her eyes to the sky, pleading for the ground to swallow her whole when her mother plodded onward. "A girl like my Jocelyn has the knowledge and training to run a household; to make a home." Juliette bit back a smile. It wasn't kind to smile at her friend's discomfort, but there was something so comforting about a mother's incessant, shameless desire to find a match for her daughter. She may have felt differently had she had a mother to mortify her or shove her in front of every remotely eligible man in their vicinity.

"I'm certain any man would benefit greatly from having a woman as lovely and kind as Miss Finchley." Ian smiled warmly, deftly evading Mrs. Finchley's none-too-subtle hint with practiced ease. Juliette wondered just how often he'd had to do something similar. No doubt he came into contact with any number of amorous ladies and their mamas; she also doubted not that she was the only one to recognize how attractive the doctor was in both mind and body.

She experienced a rapid rush of warmth when Ian's eyes found her, sweeping across her in one long, languorous caress so poignant she could feel it on every inch of her skin. Her stomach fluttered and her head felt light. It would be easy to attribute it to the sun or the fact that she'd lain awake for much of the night recalling their interlude over and over again, but there was more to it than that. So much more.

The coals smoldering in his simmering gaze promised something dark and forbidden…something that made her simultaneously tingle and ache. The sensation continued long after Ian had removed his eyes and focused on another conversation.

Eager to move onto the fishing, several of the men devoured the cold-cut sandwiches and chilled wine, picked through the variety of fruit, and then hurriedly snatched up the tackle.

Juliette smiled broadly at her brother, who looked almost boyish as he expertly fixed his pole and pawed through the basket holding the collection of shiny feathered lures and hooks and extra line, along with other implements necessary for an afternoon of successful fishing. The premature creases beside his eyes and between the bold slashes of his dark brows softened and his smile was vastly easier than it was when they were in London and Parliament was in session. He'd always been so serious, so prone to gravity and willing to take on the weight of duty, so it was relieving to see him more relaxed than she had in a long, long while. Ethan worked so hard. He was so dedicated to his political causes and the care and well-being of the tenants for whom he was responsible. Still, he found plenty of time to worry about her. Their days contained an undercurrent of concern and censure. She hadn't been lying when she'd told Ian about how her brother monitored her and did his best to ensure her health and safety by forbidding certain activities and outings.

Juliette had balked at the confinement as she grew older and less able to participate in things of which every young girl of the *ton* dreamed. All the beautiful gowns meant nothing if there was nowhere to wear them. A carriage ride through Hyde Park grated when, time after time, no suitor accompanied her, and her friends were gradually paired off with matches. She was relegated to the outskirts of the sprinkling of events she'd been able to convince Ethan to allow her to attend. Not once had she been allowed to behave like any other young woman. Ethan played the part of an overzealous guard-dog chaperone and herded her to the chairs with the rest of the wallflowers, all but snarling at any man who dared attempt to approach and ask her to dance.

She'd never danced at a ball.

Not that she'd ever been deemed well enough to learn when all the other girls her age had spent time under the tutelage of a dancing master (and, therefore, she would have made an utter fool of herself in the middle of a crowd)…but it would have been nice to have someone ask. The few interested men couldn't have possibly known how embarrassed she would have been had they managed to get past her brother—after all, who would possibly consider the daughter and sister of an earl could be lacking such a basic skill of a well-born lady?

During the perfect time of the year when the weather in London wasn't quite cloying or clogged with soot and the windows of the big houses in Mayfair were thrown open to release heated air and allow sweet, floral-scented breezes from gardens into the overstuffed rooms, music would carry on the breeze and wind its way into her home. Ethan would be at one of those events down the street or across the square, leaving her home alone. Only then, away from her brother's censure, would she spin and dance, creating her own steps to the tunes until she was dizzy and laughing, breathless with joy and not an illness. She liked to believe the twirls were graceful, that her imaginary partner thought her charming and talented. These stolen moments were her little secret. She'd felt guilty the first few times she'd done it —that she was betraying her brother by defying him and putting her health at risk—but that had gradually melted away.

After all, what point was life if there were no snippets of joy to savor like a secret sweet on your tongue?

A deep male laugh drew her attention past the men spaced out along the reedy shore, focused and intent on their fishing.

Ian.

So much of her life had been wasted waiting. She had been forced to remain passive as she watched a great many wonderful things pass her by.

As she had lain awake the previous night, she had concluded that she was done with all of that; it was well past time she rose to her feet and chased after what she wanted.

And the opportunities smoldering in Ian's eyes were just that.

*****

"Dr. McCullom," Meredith called lightly, beckoning Ian over to the blanket where she and Juliette sat, their skirts gracefully arranged and fanned out around them like halos. "Do join us."

The women watched as Ian excused himself from a conversation with Lady Morton; there was no denying the way Juliette's heart kicked up its pace as he made his way over to them. She was in awe of the innate grace with which he moved. For a man so large, he shouldn't have been able to move with such fluidity…but he did…and she was hard-pressed to look away.

Ian politely inclined his head and greeted them. She noticed he was careful not to allow his gaze to linger upon her too long.

"The folly has some interesting features I know would interest you quite greatly. I thought perhaps Lady Juliette might show them to you."

"Oh?" Juliette witnessed the fraction of a second where Lady Sommerfeld's true machinations became apparent to him. She tried not to flush. "It does appear to be quite the interesting bit of architecture. I'd be honored if our hostess would grant me a tour." He held his large hand down to her and assisted her in rising to her feet. Juliette snuck a surreptitious glance at her brother as she brushed some grass from her skirts, only to find him thoroughly engrossed in his fishing with the other men. One had just landed a respectably large pike and the others were either grousing or congratulating him. Lady Sommerfeld certainly had timed her efforts well; their absence would not be missed and, with the other guests milling about picking flowers or chatting in the shade, it was an entirely plausible excuse.

Ian slipped her arm through his and, together, they meandered in the direction of the folly.

"The folly was built by my grandfather, the Third Earl of Hopesend," she explained in a tone loud enough that it would carry to anyone nearby. "You can see the Greek influence here in the columns and the—"

Her words were effectively silenced when, as they rounded the side of the building, Ian spun them and pressed his lips and his body to hers, backing her up against one such carved column. Juliette instantly melted against him. Her knees felt like wet sand and her hands scrambled for stability with his lapels. The kiss was strong, possessive, claiming, sending a rush of liquid heat between her thighs to the very spot that had ached and throbbed throughout the long night alone in her bed. She squeezed her legs together to assuage it, but it was useless. The sensations were only heightened when Ian deepened the kiss before breaking away. Their panting breaths collided in the scant space between them.

"That was…"

"What I've wanted to do since I saw you this morning." The deep timbre of Ian's voice hummed through her chest to tickle every one of her nerve endings; his words thrilled her in unspeakable ways. More of her began to melt as her body swelled with desire. "Have you thought about what we spoke of last evening?"

Her mind moved frustratingly slowly, but she did eventually decipher Ian's words. She gave a quick nod as her mind caught up.

"And?"

"And…" Juliette's heart jumped into her throat, making her speech slower than normal. "And I want everything you'll give to me." Ian's face didn't move, but she watched the dark pools of his pupils swallow nearly every shred of the gold-flecked color of his irises and his pulse hammered in the artery of his strong throat just where it met the top edge of his cravat, his chest heaved in a shaky breath. "And, before you tell me I've not considered all of the consequences, believe that I have. I hope you would not insult my intelligence to claim I have not weighed it all and come to this conclusion."

"In that captivating mind of yours, what do you view as 'everything'?" he asked with only the hint of a waver to his tone.

All of you, Juliette nearly said before literally biting her tongue. Her mind raced to find a compromise and she then steeled her nerve to voice it aloud.

"I have never had a suitor—not that I believe you to be one, of course, I've no disillusions regarding this agreement—and I see none in my future. You gifted me with my first kiss, my first taste of… whatever this is," she tugged him a bit closer by the lapels until the heat of his body threatened to engulf her; "and I want more." Ian inhaled sharply. "I want more of these things I cannot describe. For all the books I have read and words I know in different languages, the words escape me." She felt her cheeks warm, but she persisted. "I think you like this, too. As Lady Sommerfeld said, you and I are two consenting, conscientious adults who are both in dire need of a little fun."

His lips split into the most glorious of grins and he emitted a low bark of surprised laughter. "Meredith said that, did she?"

Juliette returned his grin with one of her own. "She did. And we likely have only another minute or two before someone notices our absence. She's adept at redirection, but no one can possibly manage for that long."

"In that case…" Ian growled before dipping his head once more to kiss her deeply. Her heartbeat thrummed deafeningly in her ears by the time he pulled away. "*Cha do bhlais mi a-riamh dad cho milis,*" he breathed, the words as lilting as the breeze around them, as ancient as the ground beneath their feet.

"What does that mean?"

His wicked mouth tilted ever so slightly on the right side before he leaned in once more, his breath hot on the delicate shell of her ear. "I have never tasted anything so sweet," he translated for her in a husky tone.

"*Breugach,*" Juliette replied, unsure from where her confidence originated, but proud of herself, nonetheless.

Ian's burnished brows rose before he threw his head back in unabashed laughter. A pink cloud of pride rose within her. She had done that. She'd surprised him, impressed him, brought that smile to his face. And she'd do anything in her power to do it again.

"I assure you, Juliette, I am no liar," Ian chuckled and held her closer still. "So believe me when I say you are sweet…in so many ways. And your Gaelic accent isn't abhorrent."

"*Abhorrent?*" she snorted in a very unladylike fashion, but couldn't have cared less.

"I said it is *not* abhorrent."

"Am I supposed to accept that as a compliment?"

"Take it how you will," he replied with a smile. "But next time, say it like this…" He proceeded to show her how to pronounce the depth of the final syllable until she was able to mimic it properly.

"There." He ran his hand down her arm until he captured her fingers in his. Stepping away, he slid her arm through his once more and they resumed their stroll around the far side of the folly. "Better."

"I made a few inquiries and was able to find a Scottish maid in the employment of a friend. She spoke a few phrases and words her grandmother had taught her, but there was not much else I could learn. You are far more proficient than she."

"I am impressed by your resourcefulness."

"Reading the words can only get me so far; hearing how someone speaks the words, seeing how you form them, is vastly more helpful."

"Has the book been of interest, then?" Ian inquired lightly, turning to feign interest in a column when one of the other guests strolled away at a far enough angle to have them in view.

"Very much so," she replied, beaming. "It was yours, wasn't it? When you were a boy?"

He made a small grunt of assent but did not turn toward her.

"I shall take the best care of it and return it safely to you when I am done," she assured him, but his reply took her aback.

"It is yours," Ian said with a finality that brooked no dissent.

Juliette chewed on her lower lip, pondering this man beside her. It was obvious the waters of his soul ran quite deep.

"Oh, Lady Juliette!" Mrs. Finchley spied them and wiggled her plump fingers invitingly. Juliette raised her lace-gloved hand in acknowledgement and Ian began to guide them slowly over to the older woman.

"When will I see you again?" she whispered from the corner of her mouth.

Ian inclined his head and lowered his voice as well. "Seeing as how I am a hostage of your house party, I would assume quite presently."

Her fingers tightened on his surprisingly firm bicep in admonishment. "You know what I mean," she hissed. They were nearing the rest of the party and the lifespan of their privacy was growing short. She felt more than heard the vibration of his low, abbreviated chuckle.

"You know where to find me. If you want to learn more Gaelic, that is."

His words began to melt her joints all over again. He had offered her an open invitation.

If she dared.

Chapter Twelve

Though Ian and Juliette saw one another at supper and both partici-
pated in parlor games that evening, there was no opportunity for them
to slip away together. Still, Ian was sure she could feel the heat and
the promise of his gaze. He knew she could feel the caress of his eyes
as they trailed every curve he longed to memorize with his touch—the
recurrent pinkness of the translucent skin on her throat told him so.

Their brief interlude at the folly hadn't been enough for Ian. He
doubted anything would sate this simmering desire growing within
him for this woman. As calm and rational a person as he was, he was
far from it when she was within his reach. She couldn't possibly know
what she did to him. If she had, then she was a wise enough young

woman to give him a wide berth. Instead, she brushed past him in the parlor and stood almost within arm's reach during the ridiculous games the *ton* insisted upon playing at these house parties. This was a dangerous game they were playing.

If the earl so much as caught one of their glances or took offense to a smile, Ian's career—his very future—would go up in flames. Worse, the ramifications for Juliette had the potential to be quite severe.

Though young, the earl was not a man with whom one trifled. Juliette had told him of her brother's overprotective, almost dictatorial nature, and Ian had heard more than one story about the man's temper in Parliament. Juliette had never given Ian cause to believe her brother might harm her, but, having dealt with and treated volatile individuals in the past, it was not always something easily controlled...especially when it came to what they viewed as protection of the ones they held dearest.

Still, against his better judgment, Ian had sat up awake in the chamber he'd been assigned long after the rest of the house had retired. Every little creak of the house settling around him made his nerves jump to attention. So torturous was it that his addled mind had even contemplated seeking Juliette out...before he promptly remembered that he did not know where her chamber was located. He couldn't very well go knocking on each of the dozens of rooms on this floor and the one above it.

He could tell himself all he wanted that this arrangement with Lady Juliette was purely carnal—that he only wanted to seek her out because he desperately wanted her body—but there was more to it than that. There was more to Juliette than that.

He spent the night seething in patience, his mind and body too distracted to focus on work, until he finally drifted off in the early hours of the morning.

He did not see Juliette until the next morning when he encountered her sandwiched between the Duchess of Morton and Meredith. Snippets of the conversation answered his question as to where Juliette had been the night before. Apparently, the duchess had stayed quite late in Juliette's rooms where the women had engaged in a voracious debate about a piece of literature; at least, that was what Ian gleaned while trying not to seem too obvious.

Juliette seemed to read his mind, though. She caught his eye when he turned back to the table, shooting him an apologetic look. He returned it with a barely perceptible shake of his head. The last thing she should do is feel bad about playing the part of hostess.

The party had just begun and he had no doubt there would be many more opportunities to be had.

*****

The day was slated for hunting and it appeared the glorious weather would hold. The excitement was palpable in the buzz of chatter, the nervous tapping of polished riding boots and gloves against palms, the squeak of leather crops being twisted. The men laughed a little louder while the women adjusted their riding habits and affixed a few more pins into their hats. Much of the party, led by the earl, was to take part in the hunt, leaving behind Mrs. Finchley (too portly to properly sit a horse), Viscount Sommerfeld (sullen and grumpy over the fact that he was physically unable to participate due to his injury), Juliette (forbidden from doing so by her brother…and the fact that she'd never been allowed to take riding lessons), Ian (who had never been one for hunting or riding outside of a necessary means of transportation), and Meredith, who would stay with her husband and emphasized the fact that she had never been much good at riding (and, though it was the truth, Ian knew it was more for the fact that she was still in the early days of her pregnancy). All had been going well in that regard as far

as Ian knew and he hoped with the utmost sincerity that it would continue to do so. No one deserved happiness and a family more than
Meredith.

At one time, he'd believed he could be the man to give that to her.
He'd cared for her for many years, fancied himself to be in love with
her rather than just loving her with the loyalty and devotion borne
from years of friendship, shared experiences, and heritages. Had she
accepted him—had he not taken so long to return from the Continent
and had she not met Lord Sommerfeld—Ian didn't doubt that they
could have settled comfortably. His income would have provided
more than passably for them both and they would have built upon
their bond over their shared passion for medicine and healing. But
settling was what she would have done. He saw that now with the
clarity of a man who'd had his heart broken, or that was how it had
felt to him at the time.

There was no denying that he and Meredith cared for one another
deeply, but there was no passion there. He'd always been attracted to
her, but the same could objectively be said about any number of
women. Meredith deserved all-consuming passion, unwavering devotion, and, above all, love, and he was happy she had found it.

For that matter, was it that far-fetched that he might hope for the
same thing for himself?

Ian shook off that train of thought, not enjoying in the least how
maudlin it was turning him. If life had taught him one thing, it was
that opportunities should be snatched while they were available. Tomorrow was not guaranteed, each breath could be one's last, and all
those cliches… While a majority of his time was spent with minor
ailments, he did have significant first-hand knowledge of the fragility
of it all and had more than his share of experience with mortality.
Pondering this very thing lent a great deal of weight to his decision to

follow through with Juliette's ridiculous arrangement. He had spent decades working to live, while she had yet to truly experience life.

Just then, the dark-haired goddess of his thoughts drifted into the library where he'd been sightlessly perusing the numerous titles lining the walls for God only knew how long. He hated the way his pulse began to pound when she so much as stepped into his line of sight. Every one of his muscles contracted in anticipation, some ancient reflex ingrained so deeply he was helpless to it and could only be swept upon the crimson tide of it.

Everything else died away and his vision tunneled when she pressed the door closed with her back and slid a thick bolt home with a click that made his brain stutter.

"My brother doesn't like to be interrupted when he's working or in meetings with his solicitors," she began softly by way of explanation. Even Ian knew there were usually a couple sets of keys for the doors within a house like this; one set kept by the countess and the other by the housekeeper. The deadbolt would prevent even one with a key from entering. "His study has a similar lock. He does not like to be disturbed."

Ian could barely swallow for the painful tightness of his throat as Juliette approached him. He was sure he resembled a buck in the sights of an archer, helpless to save himself even when faced with a blatant threat to his well-being.

"Juliette," he finally managed to eke out gruffly.

"Ian," she replied with an amused tilt to her petal-pink lips. She wore her hair pulled back in several plaits and pinned in a neat coil to show off the tempting arch of her throat. The simplicity of her lilac gown with its square neckline and lace trim was demure and, yet, it managed to drive him wild. Everything about her spoke of confidence—how she leaned with one hip against the high wingback of a navy-upholstered chair, the way lifted her chin in a show of it, her steady voice—Ian knew her well enough at that point to recognize the flickers of insecurity in her crystalline eyes, but he applauded her for the demonstration of bravado. She opened her mouth once and snapped it shut before she decided to speak again. "I thought I might tell you some of the things I've learned and get your opinion."

Ian's brows rose to his hairline. Of the myriad of things that had run through his mind in the mere seconds since Juliette had entered the room, he hadn't anticipated this.

"Very well." Ian inclined his head and very politely gestured for her to take a seat. She obliged and Ian sat on the sofa beside her chosen chair. Though they were perched upon different pieces of furniture, no more than a few measly inches separated them. He was entranced by the way her dark lashes fanned across her cheeks when she looked down to adjust her skirts. She glanced up at the space beside him and sucked in a breath before she stood and, quickly enough that he wasn't allowed to rise in deference, she plopped down beside him.

"Showing you is probably easier…" Her voice in the last word trembled with the beat of her heart; further evidence to Ian that he'd read her correctly.

"Oh?"

"I began with the basics in your book. Common words and phrases." She leaned in closer and Ian inhaled her scent deeply, his eyelids involuntarily fluttering in rapture. "*Sròn*," she said with a smile as she tapped him on the nose with her finger. He chuckled. "*Cluasan*." She gently pinched the lobes of his ears between her thumbs and forefingers and he nearly groaned. He'd never before understood how the ears might be an erogenous zone, but apparently they were when Juliette did the touching… His eyes fluttered closed and then he felt her lips upon his eyelids; he fisted his hands against his thighs when she said, "*Suilean*." He stopped breathing altogether in anticipation when he felt the shaky puffs of her breath against his lips. "*Beul...*" And then her lips sealed over his.

It took less than a heartbeat's time for Ian to flip their positions and slide his tongue between her lips to sample her sweet nectar. She linked her arms around his neck and held onto him as if he was every-thing she desired in this world.

Ian was more than happy to allow himself to sink into that delu-sion.

He obliged when she tugged him closer; his hands began to peruse her curves and she sighed in surrender. The breathy little sound of surprised joy escaping her throat was his undoing. His patience and restraint had been held in check for so long by that time. He couldn't go any longer without a taste of her—without more.

He knelt on the thick rug despite Juliette's little moan of protest. "Fret not, *mo chridhe*." He placed a gentle hand on her shoulder until she relaxed and reclined, watching him with her inquisitive eyes, a swirling mixture of desire and curiosity. Sitting back on his heels, he took his time raising her skirts one delicious bit at a time. His heart raced more quickly with every inch of well-turned ankle and shapely calf clad in virginal white silk stocking gradually revealed to his rav-enous eyes. The pink lace garter ribbons, her frilly undergarments only fanned the flames burning deep within his gut.

Though she didn't stop him, he could read her insecurity in the tenseness of her creamy thighs. He began massaging her calves and gradually worked his way higher in carefully orchestrated circles. When she began to relax, he interspersed them with small kisses. They were nothing more than peppered pecks, but it was enough to make Juliette gasp and Ian's breeches grow painfully tight. She smelled better than anything he'd ever experienced. She was as clean

and sweet as a loch, as heady as heather with its complex, smoky un-
dertones. He was not a betting man, but he would wager she tasted
even better.

His body was wound so tightly that he felt as if he would combust
if he couldn't taste her properly. And soon. But he knew he needed to
take his time. She was untried and he needed to build her confidence,
not overwhelm her with the power of his desire.

"You are a treasure," he breathed, attempting to keep the tremor of
need from his voice. He slipped a fingertip beneath the edge of her
drawers as his hands crept higher. "Have you ever explored your
body?" he asked as he looked up at her from his subservient position.

The muscles in her delicate throat flexed as she swallowed.
Though the skin of her cheeks and chest fairly glowed with embarrassment, she nodded. His cock throbbed as the image of her caressing her most secret of places flashed through his mind. He couldn't
entirely silence the groan of need rumbling in his chest.

"Do not be uncomfortable. Never feel that way around me. There
is no shame in it; it is perfectly natural." Ian continued his gentle
stroking of her flesh, higher and higher. "I have done it," he admitted
boldly. "While thinking about you, in fact."

Those large eyes of hers widened even more. The way she bit her
lower lip nearly drove him mad with desire. It took every ounce of
strength within him to not spread her legs and take her right there.

His thumb caressed the springy curls at the crux of her thighs, ever
so slowly and softly creeping its way nearer to its target. She rewarded him with a shuddering sigh and her knees fell further apart. Ian
pressed an open-mouthed kiss to her inner thigh, tasting the pale skin
as sweet as sugar. His knuckle caressed the seam of her sex, now slick
with her arousal.

"How do you like to be touched, Juliette…*mo chridhe*…*mo lean-nan àlainn?*"

My heart. My beautiful sweetheart.

*****

Juliette was breathless with nervous excitement, wound so tightly that she nearly jumped up from the sofa when Ian's fingers grazed her sex. She had no chance to feel shame over the evidence of her desire had Ian not made such a guttural sound of approval.

"How shall I touch you, hm?" One of his fingers began to stroke her, parting her ever so slightly. Even that small touch made her tremble from her head to her toes. More. She wanted more. She needed it.

"Like that," she breathed so gently it was barely audible. Ian understood, and the pad of finger pressed more deeply to run from top to bottom, stroking around her entrance. Her hips canted upward to accept his touch.

"And this?" Ian asked in a voice deeper than thunder as he stroked higher to the most sensitive little pearl. And Juliette saw stars.

"Yes!" She arched into his touch, gasping and panting as he swirled through the moisture and stroked her there.

"So responsive," he murmured approvingly.

Her eyes were clenched, but she could feel his gaze upon her watching her every heaving breath and twitch of her muscles. A buzzing began to overtake her limbs, forcing liquid heat through her veins and focusing her every sense on Ian and what he was doing to her. What he was making her feel.

"And this?" The thick pad of Ian's thumb pressed into her narrow channel. She would have resisted, but the exquisite fullness combined with the consistent rhythm of his strokes made her shudder in delight.

"Oh, Ian!" Juliette whimpered and clutched at the sofa's cushions to keep her grounded. She felt as if she were near to floating away on a cloud of unspeakable pleasure.

"And will you allow me to kiss you here?" came Ian's voice, thick with what almost sounded like desperation. She unscrewed her eyes and looked down at him to be sure she'd heard him correctly. He meant to kiss her? There? The tautness around his mouth spoke of his sincerity and intense need to follow through. But she instinctively knew he would not do it without her permission.

Curiosity won out over modesty and Juliette nodded. This was all the prompting Ian needed; it took him less than a heartbeat to part the slit in her drawers and press his mouth to the dewy folds of her sex.

His kisses began very chaste, but all sense of time and place left Juliette the moment his tongue began to lick and stroke her. Her head dropped back and a moan of delighted surprise was torn from her throat when he started to nibble and caress that sensual pearl. His thumb curled within her, teasing her with little strokes and pressing somewhere that sent shockwaves of pleasure surging through her.

Gripping the sofa was no longer enough. Her hands, of their own volition, began to clutch at Ian's head and shoulders. She held him closer to her body, rocking her pelvis against him as they worked in time to urge her crisis ever closer.

"Please," Juliette sobbed. "Please, Ian." Her heart pounded and her limbs quaked. She felt as if she was climbing to a height so unfathomable she could not breathe.

And when Ian sucked deeply, she really couldn't.

Her breath was stolen from her lungs as her body curled around a silent scream. The world went black as she was consumed by pleasure, but Ian did not stop until every last tremor was wrung from her limp body. Only then did he give her relief.

After placing a damp, lingering kiss on her thigh, Ian joined her on the sofa. She allowed him to gather her in his arms and hold her against his chest where she closed her eyes and listened to the powerful thud of his heart.

Chapter Thirteen

"With all due respect, I strongly disagree." Mr. Finchley had imbibed one too many snifters of brandy following dinner and had no idea the dangerous ground upon which he trod. "Imposing such a tax will do more harm for business owners than good for the employees."

Ethan stood against the carved marble hearth, one arm slung across the mantle as his cold eyes were fixed over his guest's shoulder. Juliette knew her brother was making a valiant attempt to avoid calling Mr. Finchley any number of creative names. Having made their fortune in textiles thanks to an innovative production method, the Finchleys were considered "New Money" in London. Juliette could see how this might influence Mr. Finchley's opinions of taxation on certain exports, but that did not stop him from being wrong. Dead wrong.

Juliette had heard her brother practicing his address to Parliament enough times to quote the proposed tax. It was intended to place more money where it was most needed: In the hands of the families who worked the farms and raised the sheep, those who processed the wool and helped in the various stages of textile production. Her brother was known for his fiery oration and occasionally incendiary opinions in government, he could infuriate her when he attempted to control her life, but she knew he was a good man who wanted to use his position of power to benefit those who lacked a voice.

"I believe you are missing the point, Mr. Finchley," Lord Leighton spoke up as Ethan continued to seethe by the hearth.

"And I believe you and Hopesend are missing mine entirely," replied Mr. Finchley with a fragrant hiccup.

Juliette had to avert her head to avoid an odorous cloud of alcohol-scented words where she sat beside poor, mortified Miss Finchley. The girl was a quiet one, and, unfortunately for her, she was forever thrust into uncomfortable situations by her opinionated, outspoken, shameless parents. They weren't bad people, simply uncouth.

"Eh, Dr. McCullom," Mr. Finchley called to Ian across the room; he and Lady Sommerfeld had been listening to the back and forth in silence. Ian tipped his chin to indicate he was listening. "You're a working man, too. Help me explain to these toffs how awful their tax would be for self-made men such as us."

Ian's face grew instantly taut and Juliette could see the discomfort in his gaze. He comported himself remarkably well in these social situations, but it was another thing entirely to be placed on the spot in a potentially contentious situation.

"I am not generally one for politics—"

"Come now," chuckled Finchley; "no one else here can provide the same perspective."

A muscle flexed in Ian's jaw. Ian did not view himself as the same kind of man as Mr. Finchley. He was a man who had clawed his way out of poverty through grit and determination; while Finchley had the benefits of being born English, growing up in a comfortable family, and having the help of hundreds of underpaid hands to grow and expand his business. His business was so profitable that it had all but been handed over into the care of managers and solicitors, so the most strenuous thing Finchley had to do was sign a few papers now and again. He and his family reaped all the benefits. Meanwhile, Ian...Ian subsided on a diet of work and dreams for a better future.

Juliette held her breath, waiting to see how he would respond.

"While I appreciate your estimation of my person as a gentleman, Mr. Finchley, I fear I am technically underqualified for this label and too undereducated in the topic to provide any response worth merit." Finchley opened his carp-like mouth, but Ian cut him off. "However, having listened to this discussion now for the better part of an hour, I will say that it seems Lord Hopesend's proposed tax would greatly benefit working-class employees in England." Ethan's head turned and his eyes locked onto Ian as he continued to speak. "I am certain this seems selfish having been raised in this class, myself, but I can say with the utmost certainty that taxing businesses to assist the employees will eventually help the businesses, themselves. Giving workers a living wage will allow them to spend back into the economy. They will purchase better food, housing, and medical care—all necessities that far too many Londoners and other Britains lack."

"And how is this supposed to help the businesses, hm?" Finchley demanded.

"Healthy workers are more productive, are they not? A man who is weakened by hunger or illness cannot possibly move as quickly as one who is well-fed and hale." Ian tapped his temple. "And he is sharper when his body is well-nourished. Do you, yourself, not think better after a meal?" In response, Finchley crossed his arms over his girth. Juliette saw the corner of her brother's mouth twitch.

"This is why," Ian continued as he sat back in his chair; "I have been working to draft a plan to bring better medical care to those more remote regions. The people must still work to survive, but they cannot do so without the right resources available to them."

"Here, here!" Lord Leighton chimed in with a grin, pleased that Ian was on his side.

"And what might that entail?" Ethan asked so unexpectedly that Juliette nearly jumped.

"For one, a more standardized level of medical care to be taught and spread throughout the country. There is currently no retraining of physicians who cling to the old ways, and they are often more hindrance than help to the patients." Juliette saw Lady Sommerfeld grip her husband's hand. It seemed an entire conversation took place in that small gesture. "And it would involve traveling to those remote areas, bringing supplies and medicine, manpower to assist communities in need."

"And that would require a great deal of funding." Ethan's expression was thoughtful, and his eyes danced in contemplation.

"It would; especially because a great many of these regions may not be able to afford the same costs or resources that larger cities might. But these are people all the same, citizens of the Crown, and they all deserve the same respect and dignity afforded to anyone else."

Unexpected tears pricked the backs of Juliette's eyes. She'd had no idea the breadth of Ian's ambitions, and to hear him speak of them so passionately, so confidently, was moving. She instantly thought of what he'd told her about his father and knew from where his inspiration stemmed. He wanted to prevent children from experiencing the pain he had; he wanted to save parents from burying their babies.

How could one man devote his life to others and still wish to give more of himself? Could such a selfless man truly exist?

"Fascinating," Ethan murmured and the topic was quickly shifted to see who had traveled furthest abroad. Juliette expected it was Ian, but he remained a contentedly quiet observer.

Mr. Finchley became sullen as a child and impatiently requested another brandy from a footman.

*****

A hand darted out from a doorway just as Ian strode past. He was not, by any means, a diminutive man, but he was caught mid-step and the yank set him off balance. He stumbled to the side and into the darkened room with a grunt of surprise. The door quickly swung shut, plunging him into the shadows.

Blinded by the abrupt shift from the candlelit hallway to darkness, Ian couldn't possibly know what to expect. His muscles tensed to defend himself…until soft arms wound around his neck, fingers burrowing into his hair, and even softer lips found his in the dark. Instantly, he recognized Juliette's scent, her taste, the way she felt against him, the small sounds she made when he returned her kiss. Wrapping his arms around her slim waist, he pulled her body flush with his and tilted his head to deepen the kiss. She leaned into him, giving all of herself over to the embrace.

"I couldn't wait until tomorrow," she breathed against his lips, meeting each one of his nips and caresses with one of her own. My, how quickly she'd improved in this. Not that any of their kisses had been bad, per se, but this confidence was new. And arousing. He had to fight not to grind his hips against hers. God, what he wouldn't give to taste her again. Their interlude in the library had been transcendent, beyond anything he could have ever imagined. She tasted like honeyed mead and her soft sounds of surrender when she came would no doubt haunt him until his dying days.

His hands drifted lower to the globes of her bottom, pressing her against his rapidly growing length. She sighed when she felt the heat of his arousal pressing against the softness of her abdomen, insistent against the layers of her skirts.

He needed more.

In one swift move, Ian hiked her up into his arms, easily lifting her against him, backing her toward a dark shape that looked vaguely chaise-shaped now that his eyes were adjusting to the poor lighting. She instinctively locked her ankles around his hips and it was impossible for him not to imagine her doing that as he pounded into her, claiming her again and again as his and his alone. It was a stupid, futile thought, but if a man couldn't fantasize in the throws of passion, then what did he have?

Juliette's lips trailed along his jaw, pressing hungry, open-mouthed kisses as he lowered her to the cushions. Bracing one leg on the floor and the other knee balanced upon the chaise, he was finally able to achieve the leverage his aching body desired. He rocked against her and her every gasp drove him higher and higher. He could feel the warmth at the crux of her thighs even though the falls of his breeches and her undergarments; the friction of his rock-hard cock against the fabric wasn't what he desired, but he was so very close to what he wanted most that he almost didn't care.

Almost.

He nipped her neck, nibbling a trail down to the swells of her perfect, pert breasts. His tongue dipped below the neckline of her dress to tease the edge of her cleavage while he palmed one of her breasts, wondering silently at its excellent fit for him. Juliette arched her back and pressed herself more firmly into his touch when his thumb discovered her pebbled nipple and teased it through the fabric.

"Ian!" she gasped, her hips rotating against him. He happily obliged and used his pelvis to provide a counterpressure to her desperation.
The room around them echoed with their sighs and gasps.

Ian wanted to touch her petal-soft flesh. He longed to taste every
inch of her. She drove him mad with her coy glances and innocent
attempts at seduction. It was time she knew a fraction of what she put
him through; of the thoughts that kept him awake and aching long
into the night until he finally caved to his baser needs and brought
himself to a frustrated, unfulfilled climax.

"You're wet for me, aren't you lass?" he ground out. Her trembling
fingers stilled in his hair. "Here," he whispered harshly; "the part of
you which aches for me the most. It's wet with your need, is it not?"
He couldn't make out the details of her features, but he was certain
her fair cheeks flushed as they were wont to do. "Touch yourself." He
demanded, desperately needing her to do so—to caress her flesh in a
way he dared not, lest he lose all control once and for all. He could
live through her or perish waiting.

She hesitated until he took her hand and gently guided it lower between them. Her knuckles brushed his painfully hard arousal and his
breath hissed through his teeth. He covered her hand with his. "Here.
Tell me how wet you are." His voice lowered further. "Touch yourself
like you do only when you're alone in the dark. Or soaking in the
tub."

She took a shaky breath and cupped her sex. He sensed the weak-
ening of her resolve and the small movements of her fingers, parting
the damp petals, gently, tentatively stroking. When she released a
small moan, his body trembled. When she gasped and her pelvis undulated, pressing her against his throbbing cock, he saw stars.

His desire rumbled up from deep within his chest as he pressed his
lips to the hammering pulse in her throat. "Tell me," he commanded.

"I—I can't," she whimpered. He could hear her arousal in her voice. She may have been shy, but she was not averse at all to what they were doing.

"You can," he insisted. "You must because you coerced me into this position, you dragged me into this room, and you know damn well I cannot do all the things I want to do to you." His accent was as thick and heavy as the heated air between them. She turned her face into his throat. "I want to feel how wet I make you in your most secret of places. I want to taste you there. I want to fill you." *I want to brand you and claim you as* mine. He ground against her, pressing her hand more firmly against her body, sliding her fingers deep within her. She gasped and breathed against the hot strip of flesh beneath his jaw and above the edge of his cravat. It was pure torture. He loved and hated it at the same time. "I want to bring you pleasure until everything except my name leaves your mind." She moaned softly against him; he could feel the back of her hand working more furiously against the front of his breeches.

"Yes," Juliette breathed, her head falling back to the cushion of the chaise. Her thighs trembled around his hips. Even without touching her directly, he knew her climax was close.

"Are you wet for me?" he demanded.

He felt more than saw her nod.

"Show me."

She worked her arm and hand back up between them. His nostrils flared with the warm, honeyed scent of her arousal. Ian couldn't help it, he captured her fingers between his lips and sucked. She squealed in surprise at first, but it quickly melted away and matched his groan of delight as his tongue swirled and savored her nectar. He pressed his aching cock firmly against the moist notch of her sex, thrusting and grinding, cursing every layer of fabric between them, but knowing it was the only thing keeping him from making an irrevocable mistake.

"So delicious," he growled before catching her mouth with his, continuing his long, firm, languorous thrusts against her body. The hitch in her breathing told him he was hitting just the right angle and he continued onward, relentlessly pursuing both her pleasure and his own.

She clutched at his flexing shoulders and hooked one leg around his hips as best she could with her skirts trapped beneath her body and one of his legs.

"Ian," she sobbed, and he knew she was just there.

When she shattered beneath him, all grasping hands and trembling limbs, mouth wide in a silent scream, he tumbled after her with three more furious rolls of his hips. His orgasm began in the base of his spine, exploding from him with furious force and flying through his every limb with the most exquisite of agonies.

Eventually, Ian unscrewed his eyes and, when his vision returned as much as it was going to in the dark room, he gazed down at Juliette. There was a glint of an eye, the shadow of a smile, the pale swells of her breasts heaving above the edge of her bodice with her every panting breath.

He'd never done anything like this before, never experienced an orgasm in quite this manner, and by God, it had been glorious. He hardly cared that he'd come in his breeches like a randy lad seeing his first pair of tits. No. All he cared about was the glorious woman reaching up and cautiously cupping his cheek in her palm.

"Oh, Ian," she sighed.

And he was dangerously content.

Chapter Fourteen

Juliette's body continued to tingle the rest of the evening and into the following day. It made it particularly difficult for her to concentrate on any of the conversations bubbling around her, and she nearly sent a ball through the library window when she attempted to participate in a game of pall mall. It was decided that all would be safer if she handed over her mallet and became a spectator. It turned out she was useless at that as well because she completely forgot to clap when the game concluded. All she could think about was Ian's body covering hers and the sounds he made when he finally caught up to his release.

The memory heated her blood so quickly, so thoroughly, that she felt as if she were burning from the inside out. She barely caught herself before she began to fan her face.

As she joined the other ladies for tea, she could only think about getting Ian back into her arms.

Unfortunately, Ian excused himself from supper that evening. He sent his regrets down from his rooms, indicating that his work had suffered too much already this week. Juliette might have been concerned that she'd done something wrong—that she'd misstepped when she'd pulled him into the unoccupied second-floor room and into one of the most erotic, compromising situations she'd never dared to imagine—had she not received a separate note from him. At first, it made no sense, but it gradually became apparent that it was a code. In his absence, Ian had presented a new challenge to her in the form of a lengthy note written in lines of alternating languages.

The first line was in French, the second was incomprehensible to her. The third line was in Italian, and the fourth was again, unreadable—wait. She knew that word. *Chridhe*. It was the Gaelic word for "heart." She recognized it from the children's book Ian had gifted to her. And he'd used that word the last time they'd been together; "*mo chridhe*," he'd said. *My heart.* And there, just above that word in the third line was the Italian word for heart, *cuore*. All at once, she realized what Ian had done. He'd written her a note in simple code, using a combination of languages he knew she could speak and read. Beneath each line of that text was a corresponding translation of that phrase into Gaelic. He had given her a linguistic challenge to further her education, just as he'd promised. He was a man of his word who knew just how to tantalize her thirst for knowledge.

She admired the graceful combination of foreign letter combinations and strange little accent marks. And her heart tripped and fell so hard that she knew it would never recover.

A playful archery tournament was scheduled for the following day. Though she'd stayed up quite late working on her translation of Ian's note, Juliette looked forward to the day's event. The prize was more symbolic than an actual trophy: All the guests had raved about Cookie's rich chocolate tart, so Juliette had asked her to whip up another to go to the winner of their competition.

"Each competitor will have three arrows, one shot from each distance marker. The most consistent archer will win our delicious prize." A few men made appreciative murmurs in response to Juliette's announcement.

"When you say consistent, does that also mean the archer who misses every shot could potentially win the competition?" asked Lady Morton cheekily. "Missing all three shots is still technically consistent." Everyone chuckled, even Juliette.

"How about the archer with the most arrows closest to the center will be crowned our winner?" Juliette capitulated.

"Yes, winner of the best chocolate tart this side of the Channel!" one of the men shouted cheerfully, earning a round of approving cheers and applause.

Juliette and Ethan handed the equipment to the first archer, Lady Morton. For all her joking, she turned out to be a decent archer. Her arrows all hit the target and came within a hand's length of the center.

Miss Finchley's arrows flew less true. The first two landed shy of the hay-backed target, but the third struck the top of the target.

Lady Sommerfeld performed admirably, likely spurred on by the competitive streak she shared with her husband. Their quips in between shots provided much laughter and entertainment for the party.

Juliette was the final lady to have her turn, and Ian knew with sudden shocking intensity that he was in trouble. She held her back and forearm as straight as a pagan goddess, her chest thrust out and hips in perfect alignment. The arrow was nocked and she stood in that pose with unwavering confidence until the arrow was loosed and flew with a zing to within an inch of the target's heart.

"Brava!" the Duchess of Morton clapped excitedly; the rest of the guests quickly followed suit.

"Your sister is an impressive shot," Lord Leighton remarked appreciatively. Ian did not care for the appraisal in that tone. In even the short time of their acquaintance, Ian had learned the man never used it unless he was inspecting a particularly interesting insect. His fists clenched at his side, his teeth grinding until they squeaked beneath the pressure.

"She's a touch out of practice," the earl explained, watching while his sister prepared her next arrow. "But she is rather good. It was one of the few activities in which she had lessons." The next arrow landed even closer to the center than the first.

"Quite good. And her form is lovely," interjected another of the guests…Baron Something-Or-Other. Ian had not bothered to commit the man's name to memory since the baron had demonstrated even less interest in getting to know Ian. Now, Ian was glad of it, because it would make killing the man all that much easier.

Juliette's last arrow struck home and it was quickly followed by enthusiastic applause. Juliette strode over to the earl and poked him in the chest. "Prepare to lose, just like when we were children."

"Hardly," Hopesend laughed in reply before striding over with the larger bow and setting up for his turn.

Juliette stopped at Ian's side under the pretense of watching her brother. She stood with her arms crossed and it took everything in Ian to not look down and appreciate the swells of flesh above the neckline of her emerald green gown, especially now that he knew how that flesh tasted.

"I'd no idea what a markswoman you were," Ian murmured, never taking his eyes off the earl.

"I thought it might be a deterrent if you discovered I could find a hare's eye from across a field."

"Can you?"

He loved the way her lips curled. "In theory. I've hit such a target, but I never had the stomach for actual hunting—not that I would have been allowed to anyway."

He and Juliette joined in the polite congratulations when the earl completed his turn and passed the bow along to Leighton.

"My father taught me to hunt when I was a lad," he said in a low tone.

"With a bow?"

Ian shook his head. "A slingshot."

"Indeed?"

"Like you, I didn't care much for the killing, though I became quite adept at catching small game for supper."

"That's because you're a healer and a provider."

Ian turned to Juliette, but her face gave no hint of the depth of the words she'd just spoken—as if she hadn't just touched a deep, guarded part of his soul. He swallowed past the burgeoning lump in his throat and returned his attention to the competition in time to watch Mr. Finchley's arrow soar five feet above the top of the target.

"Your go, McCullom." The baron offered the bow to Ian.

"I fear my skills will be sorely lacking," Ian said with a self-deprecating chuckle.

"I would be glad to give you a quick lesson, Dr. McCullom." Was it Ian's imagination, or had Juliette shot a very pointed glance in Lady Morton's direction?

No. Ian had been correct.

The duchess caught the earl's attention with a delicate hand. "Your aim is rather impressive, Lord Hopesend. Might I trouble you for a lesson as well?" Juliette's brother could not decline, nor did he seem to want to when faced with the beautiful duchess's charms. In fact, she was almost too adept at garnering male attention, because every man in attendance quickly sought to provide his tips and assistance with her lesson. It was a remarkable trick, Ian had to admit that much.

Juliette cleared her throat and gestured for him to follow her to the first distance marker. With nearly everyone else distracted, Juliette and Ian were left fairly alone.

"You are quite a bit larger than I, so the bigger bow will be better suited to you." Ian's hand tingled when her bare palm grazed his in the transfer. He nearly shivered when she traced his palm and showed him how to position his fingers on the string. "You must be at once firm and flexible."

"That does not make sense."

"Of course it does. One must strive to be both firm and flexible in all situations."

"*All* situations?" Ian asked beneath his breath, thrilled by the subtle reaction he earned from her.

She cleared her throat daintily before replying. "Yes. All situations. Now, let me show you the proper stance."

Ian immediately moved to imitate the position in which he'd seen Juliette and the others stand, but her light little laugh was proof that he was severely lacking in his mimicry.

"Here. Like this." Juliette stood behind Ian and used her foot to nudge his feet further apart. An involuntary groan rose in his throat when she gripped his hips in her small hands and turned his pelvis. The blasted lass knew precisely what she did when she ran her fingernails up his sides and she pressed her breasts to his back. Thankfully, the rest of the guests were behind where they stood, so it appeared to them, for the most part, that Juliette was providing innocent guidance to him. There was, however, anything but innocence in the way she stroked his clenching abdomen and caused his breath to hiss through his teeth.

"You're playing a dangerous game, Juliette," Ian gritted out through his teeth.

"Of course." He could hear the smile in her voice. "Archery can be quite dangerous." She was being purposefully obtuse and it drove Ian mad with frustration and need. He wanted to reverse their roles; he longed to hold her back to his front with her curves nestled against him; he wanted to fit himself against the round curves of her bottom and—

"Now, practice pulling back the string. That's it." One of her hands braced his stationary shoulder while the other cupped his moving bicep, very clearly enjoying the play of muscle beneath the fabric of his coat. "And when you release, allow it to happen." She couldn't possibly be alluding to— "A proper release can be the most satisfying thing in the world."

Ian turned his eyes to Juliette but continued facing the target. "Where has this minx come from?" he growled from low in his chest.

"She's been here all along," Juliette said, gently correcting the height of the bow he held. "No one else saw her before." The last was added in a whisper, something so soft and delicate Ian might have believed it as intangible as a dream.

He saw her.

All of her.

Ian witnessed the brilliant woman with a passion for foreign tongues. He saw her sense of humor and her easy smile. He saw her shy side and her sensual side. Her mischievous side and her sweet side.

And he wanted all of it. Ian wanted all of her.

He'd been irredeemably ignorant believing he could walk away from this arrangement unscathed. He'd known it from the first time he'd looked into Juliette's eyes on that London street that she would be his undoing.

"Feel the wind," Juliette said in a smooth return to his archery lesson…as if she hadn't shaken his world like an earthquake of extraordinary magnitude. "You will need to adjust your aim as it will carry your arrow.

Ian could sympathize with the arrow. He'd been carried off to places unknown just as helplessly as if he were a bit of stick and feather at the mercy of nature.

*****

Ian was staring at the papers spread out before him but saw none of them. He'd retreated to the safety of his chamber following luncheon under the guise of getting more work done, but it was futile. Especially when he realized his coat smelled like Juliette from having her pressed so near.

He'd performed just about as poorly as to be expected when it came time for him to shoot an actual arrow, but Juliette's smile had been well worth the good-natured unmanning he'd received.

Now, instead of reviewing potential costs for ordering cloth strips, silk thread, and other basic medical necessities in bulk, Ian's groin pounded with furious need. He suffered from an insatiable hunger for Lady Juliette Crawford.

Ian's brows knit together following a small scratch at the door. He hadn't sent for anything and none of the other guests had reason to disturb him. His heart kicked up instantly at the possibility that it might be Juliette, but surely she was not foolish enough to seek him out in the middle of the day when anyone might stumble upon her.

He would have lost that bet, however, because he opened the door to find her wide blue eyes and perfectly kissable lips waiting for him on the other side.

"Juliette?" Ian croaked disbelievingly.

"I thought you might like some chocolate tart," she said, holding up the plate in her hand. Sure enough, there was a thick slice of the decadent desert waiting for him. "Even one of the worst marksmen of the day deserves a little something sweet." He nearly groaned, because she couldn't have known how he'd so recently imagined *her* being that something sweet, laid out across his bed like a desert spread for him alone.

"You shouldn't be here," was all he managed to say.

"I am just delivering your conciliatory prize and I shall be on my way...leaving your virtue intact." The glitter in her voice finally snapped Ian's restraint.

He hauled her into his room and had just enough sense to drop the plate on the desk with a clatter before hauling her against him and kissing her with every ounce of longing he'd held in check for the interminable hours since the last time they had touched.

"You are the sweetness I crave," he growled between kisses. His tongue stroked her mouth deeply, exploring, tangling with hers in a furious dance.

She pressed her lower body against his, gasping when she felt the rigid evidence of his need. He couldn't resist the testing thrust his hips made against her softness. Painfully hard and desperate for her touch, Ian captured one of her hands and brought it to his groin, holding her palm there to cup him through his breeches.

"Do you feel what you do to me, lass," he growled, grinding into her. "I've been hard since you teased me during archery…and I'm no' a man to trifle with."

"Show me." Juliette's words were muffled against his lips, but there was no mistaking them. Especially not when she squeezed him in the most delicious grip.

Panting, Ian freed his throbbing member, and Juliette's hand immediately covered it with soft, exploratory fingers.

"So good," he hissed. "I've wanted your hands on me for so long, lass." And one of his fantasies was realized when she knelt in front of him and began to stroke.

"It's quite beautiful," Juliette said in a shaky voice. He could practically feel her appreciative eyes upon the thick, ruddy head. Her hand tested the girth and length next, trying to see if her fingers would meet as she wrapped them around him tightly, stroking where the root sprung from a nest of reddish curls. He moaned in delight, knowing her virgin flesh would be even more tantalizingly tight than this. He fought not to thrust into her, lest he break the spell of the moment.

"Not half as beautiful as you." Juliette's face flushed; he suspected his did as well when she looked up at him from that position, her beautiful eyes wide and her hand on his cock.

"May I kiss you?" she asked softly, and it nearly brought Ian to his knees.

"Please," was his strangled reply. And Ian nearly died when he watched her grip his member reverently and place a very tender, chaste kiss upon one of the least chaste places he possessed. And he never wanted it to end. He nearly lost consciousness when she did it again and her lips parted, tongue darting out to trace the slit.

"Fucking hell…" he groaned and his fingers flew to her head; his heart thudded so hard against his ribs it made them ache.

He wanted to hold her there.

He wanted to thrust deep as she sucked him.

He wanted to watch her delight as he poured out his soul and surrendered to her completely.

Instead, he held so utterly still, afraid to breathe or move lest she disappear into smoke.

She rewarded him with another kiss. And then another. And another. Growing bolder and more comfortable with each one until she enveloped his aching head between her lips, sucking tentatively.

It nearly killed him to do it, but Ian forced himself to speak: "You needn't do that."

"I want to…"

And that was his undoing. He helped her find a rhythm with her kisses and caresses. She took him deeper, learning how a flick of her tongue could make him lose his breath, and a swirl around the head made him weak in the knees.

The groan ripped from his chest was animalistic, layered with amazement and disbelief at what she was gladly doing to him. Ian basked in the glow of her attention, the selfless way she wanted to learn to give him pleasure. His head fell back in surrender, his chest heaving as the strength of his arousal increased. It rose within him swiftly and violently, building at the base of his spine and ricocheting through his limbs, washing his mind free of everything except for her hands, her mouth on him. And when her free hand cupped the soft sac beneath his member, Ian knew all was lost.

"*Mo leannan àlainn*," he gasped roughly. "You must stop."

She did so instantly, removing her mouth and gazing up at him with wide, concerned eyes. "Did I hurt you?"

"No," he said with a shake of his head. His thumb stroked the curve of her cheek. "It feels far too good."

"Oh." Her eyes returned to his aching cock, so hard it was painful as it strained for release. And then, Juliette did the unthinkable, she leaned in and took him into her mouth once more, redoubling her efforts.

He cursed in English, Gaelic, Italian, and likely several other languages as he careened helplessly toward his orgasm. His vision blurred and his fingers knotted in her hair, holding her still as his thighs trembled and his cock throbbed in release, pouring into her his hot seed as waves of pleasure rolled through him like an unstoppable tide.

As the last tremors left his body, he dropped to his weakened knees and cupped her face in his large hands, pressing his forehead to hers. Their panting breaths mingled between them.

"Did I do well?" Juliette asked softly.

In response, Ian kissed her deeply, tasting the salty musk of his release on her tongue and savoring it.

Chapter Fifteen

Juliette's hands were less than steady at supper that night. She couldn't prevent her mind from replaying her encounter with Ian again and again. Seeing him so uninhibited, so wild was thrilling. Realizing she was able to have him at her mercy and bring him to his knees was overwhelming.

Her untried mind had never before pondered what it would be like to take a man in her mouth, but she hadn't been able to resist when confronted with the impressive beauty of Ian's arousal. Something deep and primal within her knew she had to have him inside her; she was driven to return the pleasure he'd given to her.

And she had loved it.

It was a foreign act, but one she would not mind repeating—not when Ian praised her and so obviously cherished her efforts.

She wondered if this was the bloom of love...this desire to step out of one's usual life and comfortability for the sake of another's joy...to derive one's joy and pleasure from that of another. The feeling was at once humbling and thrilling. It made her want more. And it was what drove her to decide that she would give herself fully to Ian that night.

She had not come to this decision lightly, but she'd be lying if she claimed she hadn't considered the possibility since they had first made their arrangement. How could a woman not wonder what it would be like to be forever ruined by a man such as him?

The very thought made Juliette's throat tight and her palms sweat.

He'd given her so many tastes of pleasure, but they had only whetted her appetite. She wanted Ian to claim her utterly and completely. Irrevocably. She could live a century, her brother could decide to throw open the doors and allow her into a world of endless suitors, and Juliette knew she would never meet another man like him.

And she loved him.

Despite his words that melted her body and soul; despite his care and worship of her body; despite his undeniable ability to listen to her and go out of his way to show her he thought of her, Juliette was keenly aware that he likely did not feel the same. Ian was an honorable man who had compromised those morals for her. She might have felt guilty about it had she not known they'd both derived so much pleasure from their time together.

She was still determined to hold up her part of the bargain. She'd promised Ian that their arrangement would be only temporary. It might break her, but she was determined to keep her word...after she experienced what it was to be skin-to-skin with this amazing, beautiful Scotsman.

Juliette smoothed the pleated skirt of her ice-blue gown and adjusted the strings of pearls and dangling aquamarines at her throat. The neckline was one of the more daring ones she'd commissioned just that Season. Normally, she opted for more comfortable, serviceable styles since she was so rarely in situations where she would require the extra flare and attention. She was glad she'd listened to that little voice in the back of her head a few months prior, however, when her modiste had presented her with the fashion plate and Juliette had instantly listened to her gut and daring gown was now hers.

The color had been chosen to highlight the brightness of her eyes and stand in even more striking contrast to the rest of her coloring. She felt ethereal. She felt unexpectedly confident. Perfect for a seduction and one scandalous night of passion.

"I adore the theater," Miss Finchley said shyly after a sip of her wine. Ian had been seated between the young lady and her mother, much to the delight of the matchmaking Mrs. Finchley.

The poor girl had leaned over as soon as her mother was occupied by an inquiry presented by Lord Leighton to her left and apologized to Ian for her mother's rather tactless behavior. He'd instantly assured her that no apologies were necessary; he was quite used to these efforts and was unfazed by them. The young lady was quite pretty when she smiled. She had a pleasantly plump face and dark eyes that lit from within when she smiled. She was also a very interesting conversationalist when one or both of her parents weren't talking over her. He sincerely hoped she would find herself a good match so she could be free of her parents; Ian, however, could not be that man. He'd cast a glance up the table where Juliette sat beside her brother, looking resplendent in a gown as blue as a crisp spring sky.

For now, he would enjoy Miss Finchley's company and give the girl an evening of pleasant conversation without subtext or hidden agenda.

"Have you seen any recent productions?" Ian asked her. "I fear my schedule does not permit me to attend the theater as much as I would like, but I do enjoy hearing about it."

This proved to be quite the right topic of conversation for the normally reserved Miss Finchley. She instantly launched into a description of Drury Lane Theatre's most recent dramatic interpretation of *Richard III*.

"Edmund Keane is remarkable," she breathed. "He has such a way of playing the despicable villain. He surely must be one of the most emotionally expressive actors of our time—aside from Garrett Frost, of course."

"Frost?" Ian frowned as he sifted through his memory. "He is with The Mask & Lyre, is he not?"

"Indeed, he is. I saw him perform the lead in *Hamlet* this Season and it was quite the performance. I confess I cried right there in the theater for his poor tortured soul."

"It must have been quite the experience," Ian said with a kind smile.

"Oh, it certainly was!"

Just then, he caught Juliette watching him. He met her eyes and, rather boldly, refused to be the first to look away. Heat crackled and sparked between them, instantly causing his breeches to grow too tight and his pulse to throb in his skull. Deep inside, something roared to life and demanded satisfaction. It wanted to sink inside of Juliette over and over again and keep her with him always. It was futile. It was foolish. But there was no reasoning with that slumbering beast now that it had been awakened.

One of Juliette's perfectly shaped dark brows rose in a question and Ian replied with a subtle inclination of his head. Whatever it was, he would walk through fire for her.

Ian turned his attention back to Miss Finchley to continue their conversation about plays and dramatic productions.

Ian stood outside a wide mahogany door, its polished brass knob so shiny he could see a warped version of his reflection staring back at him. His heart was pounding fitfully, almost concerningly, as he debated whether to knock or listen to his better judgment and walk away.

His left hand held the small scrap of parchment, upon which had been written Gaelic instructions to this very room. The note had been slipped to him beneath Juliette's curled fingers as he'd bent over her hand to bid her goodnight.

He'd been surprised to feel it hidden there, but he'd masked his reaction and accepted it before secreting it into an inner pocket of his coat. He'd excused himself for the evening very soon thereafter and escaped into the hall to read it.

Staidhre an t-seirbhiseach. An treas làr. An ceathramh doras air an taobh chlì. Meadhan oidhche.

Ian's breath had died in his lungs. *Servant's stairs. Third floor. Fourth door on the left. Midnight.*

He'd spent the next hour-and-a-half pacing his room in indecision and anxiety. She wanted to see him, that much was clear, but what did it mean? What did she hope would happen?

The previous day in his rooms had been their most private of interludes, but it had also been spontaneous. She had some plan in that beautiful head of hers, and Ian was unsure whether or not he should go through with it…especially now as he was realizing the depth of his feelings for her. This could only lead to disaster.

But his body did not seem to agree. At three minutes to midnight, Ian's legs carried him from his room to the disguised doorway leading to the servants' stairwell. He climbed the narrow flight to the floor above his where the family rooms lay. He didn't remember counting the doors, but he found himself face-to-face with the one behind which held one of his greatest desires.

He raised his hand and rapped one knuckle on the doorframe.

*****

Juliette's heart stopped at the slight knock on the door to her bedchamber. She'd hoped to hear it. She'd been waiting for nearly two

hours for it. But, now that it had happened, it was as shocking as gun-
fire beside her head.

She had to shake herself and force her feet to move. She'd asked
for this; she had dreamt about it. Nothing else had occupied her mind
beyond imagining that moment when she found Ian standing there
waiting for her.

His head was tilted in a charmingly unsure way—as if she hadn't
been the one to invite him there, to have been the one to provide him
with directions to where she awaited. She hooked a finger in his
waistcoat and tugged him forward, closing the door behind him.

His breathing was shaky as she guided him further into the rose-
colored room.

"What am I doing here, Juliette?" Ian rasped as she slipped her
hands into his. Despite his words, he wove their fingers together.
There was something so achingly sweet about it—a familiarity she'd
never even considered and now realized she did not wish to live without.

"My education is lacking in one area," Juliette began, hoping her
voice was steadier than her stomach.

"Your note was well done."

"I do not mean my Gaelic." Ian's mouth snapped shut; the knot in
his throat bobbed. "I know there is more I do not know, and I wish to
know all of it."

"This is not something that can be undone."

"Have I once shown any regret for anything we have done, Ian?"
He averted his eyes and she knew his resolve was waning. She was
winning. "I will not regret this either."

"I am not the man—"

"You are *exactly* the man...the *only* man I want this with." She
brought his hand to her face and pressed a lingering kiss to the palm.
His eyes shuttered and his lips parted. She could practically scent his
desire on the air. "Unless you do not want this."

Ian yanked her to him with a suddenness that made her gasp. His thick thumb traced her lower lip. "Lass. I've wanted nothing more in my life…and I've dreamt of nothing else since kissing this mouth of yours."

She would have told him she hadn't either, but his lips slanted over hers, his tongue sliding home to dance and tangle and claim her breath and her heart as his.

Juliette was suddenly grateful that, for once, Fanny had been so quick to help her prepare for bed because her nightdress provided little barrier to Ian's heat. She could feel every one of the muscles in his chest and abdomen ripple as he worked to divest himself of his coat. His waistcoat and cravat followed soon after, tossed away to land on the floor, her desk, and a chair. She barely had time to examine the hard planes of his body before he crushed her to him once more. Both their hands caught and dragged, squeezed and caressed, memorized every curve and hollow, earning gasps of delight and moans of pleasure.

Soon, her nightdress was pulled high enough that Ian's giant hands could palm the globes of her bottom. He gripped her tightly, pulling her closer while simultaneously grinding his pelvis against her. She recognized the thick, hard ridge of his arousal and her knees nearly buckled. It had been one thing to be in control when she touched him and kissed him there; it was another to surrender to him and completely give herself and her body to him. She longed for it, but it was also as frightening as it was exciting.

Ian lifted her in one easy movement, hiking her against his chest and pulling her thighs around his waist. Juliette's head dropped back as he began to nip and nuzzle the length of her bare throat.

"You've no idea how long I've wanted to be between these long legs," he panted against her skin, sending a shiver of appreciation through her body. "Tasting you was glorious, but feeling you wrapped 'round me, squeezin' me tight as I fill you…aye, that'll be heaven."

A whimper was ripped from her throat as he set her on the edge of the bed.

"*Tha thu bòidheach*," he murmured while gazing down at her, his eyes skimming over her face, then the pale shoulder exposed by her slipping gown, the swells of her heaving breasts with their erect, dusky nipples pressing against the thin fabric. And she certainly felt as beautiful as he claimed her to be.

He knelt before her like an ancient warrior for his queen and slowly raised the hem of her nightshift higher to expose the tops of her creamy thighs and the thatch of dark hair protecting her sex. She might have been embarrassed had she not already known how much he enjoyed her body, the things he could do to her and the way he could make her feel.

Cheekily, she leaned back on her elbows to look down her body at his chestnut hair, burnished nearly fiery red in the dim candlelight, and spread her thighs wide. His gorgeous irises were nearly swallowed whole by their pupils as he surveyed her most secret of places with what could only be described as unabashed admiration.

"Perfection," Ian groaned and spread her with his thumbs before dipping his head to lick the dew gathering in the folds of her sex.

Lips parted in a silent cry of joy, Juliette could only give in to the flames of desire and allow herself to be slowly consumed by them. Her hips jerked involuntarily, grinding her body against Ian's wicked mouth and spurring him on.

"Aye. That's it," he mumbled into her body before doing something quite wicked with his tongue. "Use me for your pleasure. *Is ann leatsa a tha mi*." *I am yours*. A shuddering sigh escaped her when he hauled her closer and propped his shoulders beneath her thighs; his tongue prodded deeply, swirling and tasting. Her legs clamped around his head, and she began to sob his name, her crisis building ever stronger within her, gathering speed and intensity as he continued his onslaught. She felt pulled taut and plucked to within a razor's edge of snapping. Her body was no longer under her control; she had become a bundle of nerves and pulsating pleasure beneath the masterful ministrations of the man feasting upon her flesh. She knew he would not stop until she reached her pinnacle. The knowledge that he was wholly dedicated to her pleasure was what set her over that edge.

Every muscle in her body throbbed with her release, from the inside out. Stars shot across her vision and she was unable to catch her breath in between cries of ecstasy.

"Ian. Ian!" Juliette rode wave after wave of her orgasm, soaring so high she barely registered when he rose and, having released himself from his breeches, rubbed the broad head of his sex through her wetness and pressed forward.

She felt her body stretch and give as he nudged deeper with every clench and release of her inner muscles. Her climax melted away and, recognizing the intrusion, her body began to resist. Her hands flew to Ian's arms braced on either side of her and she gripped him, unsure if she was urging him on or begging him to stop.

Ian's eyes met hers. His chest, sprinkled with red-gold hair, heaved with the intensity of his restraint.

"I ken it's uncomfortable," he said, his voice slipping into a thicker Scottish accent than she'd heard before. "But this is necessary. It will no' hurt so much after this. I promise." The sincerity in his eyes comforted her, but it was the tautness of his features that made her decide to allow him to continue. He was desperate to continue, but he hated the fact that she was in pain and would stop if she asked him to; she knew it in her heart.

Juliette nodded and held onto Ian, trusting him as he continued to press forward until his thick length was fully seated inside, stretching her beyond what she thought was her limit.

They held still together then, two bodies merged and panting as one.

"Are you well?" Ian asked, voice more strained than she had thought possible.

Juliette nodded against his damp throat and he began to move. What started as short, gentle thrusts gradually increased as she acclimated to the foreign sensations he unleashed within her. Her muscles gradually began to melt, as did her core. She could feel the dripping moisture ease his way as each thrust was smoother than the last. He kissed her then, his tongue mimicking the gentle, deep thrusts of his manhood, and she wrapped her arms around his neck, her legs falling wide to accept his hips.

"Better?"

"Yes," she replied, then gasped as he angled himself differently. "Oh, yes."

Ian's head dipped lower to follow the neckline of her nightshift. Tugging it down, his mouth closed over her sensitive nipple and she cried out in surprise. Her hands flew to his hair and held him there, every flick of his tongue plucking a new string tied from that puckered bud to her center.

"Yes," she moaned, lifting her hips to meet his thrusts. She wanted more. More. "*Tuilleadh*," she demanded. And he gladly obliged.

Releasing her nipple, Ian rose above her and braced his feet on the floor. Wrapping his arms around her legs, he tilted her just so and spread her open for both their pleasure. He increased the speed of his grinding thrusts, his soft sac gently slapping against her bottom in an unexpectedly tantalizing way. His thumb found that little nubbin at the crux of her sex and rubbed in the swirling rhythm he'd learned she favored.

Juliette closed her eyes and allowed herself to be carried away by her other senses. The room became humid with their panting breaths and sweat from exertion. The sound of gliding flesh and harsh inhalations filled her ears. She adored the feel of Ian's muscles rippling beneath his skin, the thick fullness of him pounding between her thighs, and the moist glide of his fingers as he teased her. Her fingers clawed at the coverlet to keep herself grounded, but it was futile. Her vision blurred and she could tell it was not long before she soared once more. Her body trembled uncontrollably.

"Aye." Ian continued thrusting. She unscrewed her eyes and decided the sight of his golden body with its hard planes and a light dusting of hair working over her and his eyes riveted on the spot where their bodies joined was the most erotic image in the world. "Good lass. Come again for me. I want to feel it."

Juliette was a chess piece knocked from a table. She tumbled over that otherworldly precipice and would have screamed had Ian not covered her mouth with his to swallow her joyful cries. He thrust into her hard and jerkily several more times before spilling himself inside of her with hot ropes of ecstasy, his body convulsing over hers with guttural moans.

Juliette recovered first and kissed the salty sweat from Ian's corded neck, stroking his damp back with languid fingers, and found herself wishing the moment would last forever. If only they could shut out the rest of the world and its complications and restrictions, if Ian felt the same way she did, Juliette believed in her soul that they could truly be happy.

Chapter Sixteen

Ian held Juliette close after their lovemaking. They had both stripped off what remained of their clothing and lay skin-to-skin beneath her bed's quilted coverlet. He savored her nearness and the way she overwhelmed all of his senses in the most delicious of ways. He loved the way she felt, the way she smelled, the little contented sounds he made in the aftermath of her climaxes.

The beat of their hearts mingled where their chests were pressed together. A wandering thumb ran up and down the impossibly soft flesh of her upper arm; her fingers did the same, stroking lazy patterns in the dusting of hair on his chest.

Their peace was disturbed, however, when a frantic knock sounded at the door. Both of them shot upright as if launched from a catapult.

"Lady Juliette!" Ian recognized the frantic voice of the Duchess of Morton. He glanced back to catch sight of Juliette's wide, shocked eyes. It had to be near two in the morning at that point. Whatever had precipitated this interruption was surely urgent.

Another round of insistent knocking echoed in the otherwise silent room.

"One moment!" Juliette called, gathering the sheet around her nakedness.

"You must hurry," the duchess hissed. "Viscount Sommerfeld... he's—"

There were three hard pounds from a closed fist as Lady Morton's words were cut off. Juliette scrambled to locate her nightshift and dressing gown.

"I know McCullom is in there, and I am coming in. You'd best be decent." The viscount's voice was dangerously low and urgent.

Hardly a second passed before Juliette's door flew open with a bang—she must have forgotten to lock it in her haste to be with him.

Immediately, Ian shifted to shield Juliette with his body, heedless of his nakedness. Truth be told, he would have expected the earl to arrive to exact his revenge for Ian defiling his sister rather than Sommerfeld standing in the doorway, disheveled and wild-eyed, barely dressed in a shirt and breeches. His piercing green eyes swept the scene but flew from Juliette to Ian's face as soon as they registered her state of undress as she clutched the coverlet to her chin.

To Ian's surprise, rather than berate them or threaten to tell the earl that they'd been discovered alone in a very compromising situation, Sommerfeld thrust the head of his cane at Ian.

"No less than a dozen servants have been trying to locate you for thirty minutes," Sommerfeld snarled. "Meredith is bleeding." His voice broke on the last word and Ian's stomach plummeted, his limbs went cold. "And hysterical. She refuses to say anything beyond sending me to locate you. Specifically you. What the bloody hell is going on?"

Ian's mind raced with possibilities. If there was any hope remaining, he needed to act quickly.

"Have someone retrieve my black medical bag from my room," he ordered as he slipped on his breeches and punched his arms through the sleeves of his linen shirt. "It should be on the chair by the window."

"Would you mind telling me what is going on?" Sommerfeld growled, fear and anger coloring his tone in equal measures.

"I cannot divulge anything until I examine the patient."

Juliette gasped behind him when Sommerfeld snatched the front of Ian's shirt, jerking him forward in a remarkable show of strength.

"Are you saying you won't tell me what is wrong with my wife? This is *Meredith*." Sommerfeld was appealing to Ian's longstanding affection for the girl Meredith had once been, and the connection he shared with the woman she had become. Ian refused to grow flustered—he would do no one any good if he allowed his nerves to take over. She was a patient like any other. He could not think of how devastated she would be if this pregnancy failed.

"I know." He tightened his jaw against the concern welling up inside of him and gripped the viscount's forearm in a tight fist. "You must allow me to do my job." He didn't want to harm the man—Ian knew Sommerfeld only acted out of concern for his wife—but he would do whatever was needed to do his duties to the best of his ability.

Sommerfeld must have finally believed him because he removed his hands from Ian's shirt and limped rapidly from the room, tugging the door shut behind him and bellowing for a servant.

"What is happening, Ian?" came Juliette's small voice behind him. He turned to face her face, her crystalline eyes round with worry in her pale face, though her ivory cheeks retained a touch of pink from their lovemaking. How much had changed in so short a span of time…

"I must see to Lady Sommerfeld."

"She will be alright?"

"I must go. Now," was all the answer Ian could provide.

"Right, of course. Go!" She shooed him from the room, already standing to dress.

Ian ran down the hallway toward the stairs and the sound of rapid footsteps underscored by Sommerfeld's helpless snarls.

"I am so sorry," Lady Morton ducked into her room as soon as Ian left. She was dressed for sleep in her white nightshift and cobalt blue dressing gown. Her long blond hair was plaited down her back and, though it was an absurd observation at such a time, Juliette realized how young she looked. The duchess was usually so outspoken and confident, but, at that moment, she looked impossibly young. It was difficult to remember she was not even thirty years of age when she commanded such a great degree of respect from every room into which she strode. "I heard a commotion in the hallway and discovered the viscount in a great degree of distress. He was roaring at a poor maid who'd said Dr. McCullom was not in his rooms, nor had anyone located him in any other part of the house or grounds," she explained as she quickly helped Juliette into her dressing gown. "He explained that something was wrong with Meredith…and I had a good idea of what you'd planned when I saw the looks you two shared…and then Ian was impossible to locate…" Juliette's cheeks burned and she turned her eyes down to the tie at her waist. "Please forgive me. It was the only thing I could think of to do. I tried to convince Sommerfeld to allow me to retrieve Ian, but he would not hear of it. I ran here as quickly as I could, but the man can be surprisingly agile."

"You did what you had to," Juliette reassured the duchess and covered her cold hand with her own. "Our friend's health is more important than anything, no matter what happens."

Lady Morton's mouth thinned into a grim line and she nodded in agreement with a squeeze of Juliette's hand.

Together, they dashed down the hallway and one floor down toward the rooms she'd assigned Lord and Lady Sommerfeld. As expected, there were a couple of maids taking turns leaving and arriving, carrying with them items Ian requested or running off to gather something else. It didn't escape Juliette's notice that there was also a pair of footmen barring Lord Sommerfeld from the room. And, judging from his furious, frantic pacing, the angry pounding of his cane with every halting step, Sommerfeld wasn't the least bit pleased to be kept away from his wife.

"Lord Sommerfeld," Juliette injected steel into her spine and approached him as one would a dangerous predator. She had come to know him well enough to have a sense of the depth of love he had for Meredith. He moved like a caged lion kept separate from everything that mattered to him. The weight of his adoration, fear, and concern for his wife was so powerful and beautiful that it was nearly frightening. His handsome features were pale and taut with anxiety when he whirled on her. His eyes raked her up and down as if his mind needed a moment to recognize how she fit into this tragedy. Her cheeks burned furiously when she remembered how he had found her and Ian, but she did her best to set it aside. What he must think of her… "Dr. McCullom is with her, I'm sure he won't allow anything to happen."

"I don't understand what is going on," he croaked, shaking his head. She watched his eyes shadow as his mind began to travel to an impossibly dark place. She could easily guess the panicked questions running through him: What if something happened to his wife? What if there was nothing Ian could do? Even Juliette understood that the blow of losing his wife would undoubtedly be the end of the viscount—she'd learned that he'd teetered on the brink after his injury and had isolated himself from Society and only his wife had been able to heal him enough to bring him back to life.

Juliette was at a loss. What did one say to a man so terrified?

"Juliette? What are you doing here?" She hadn't spotted Ethan around Lord Sommerfeld's shoulder, so concerned she'd been about the viscount's state of mind. Her brother looked as if he'd been roused from sleep as well and was dressed similarly to the viscount in nothing more than a linen shirt and breeches, his dark hair uncharacteristically tousled.

"I—I…" She felt her face lose all its color in a rush of panic. Her mind froze. She was saved from having to answer when the door opened and Ian stepped from the room.

Juliette recognized in the hard mask of his face that he'd donned his physician's persona, surgically separating his emotions from his work. Gone was his tender passion and the sweet smile she experienced only a short time ago; his eyes were unreadable, his mouth a fine, impassive line.

Juliette braced herself, twisting her fingers together until they were white and growing numb. It was nothing compared to the stillness that took hold of Sommerfeld. The servants scampered away and tension filled the hallway around the five of them. Lady Morton came up beside her and held her hand. Ian cast a glance in Juliette's direction before stepping closer to Sommerfeld. She was torn between allowing them privacy and wanting to be near in case the news was grim; Juliette knew Meredith wouldn't want her husband alone if that were the case.

Ian inclined his head to the viscount's and spoke in a low, steady tone. Sommerfeld flinched and heaved a sigh which quickly morphed into a sob. His cane clattered to the floor and he sank to the ground more quickly than was comfortable, but he didn't seem to notice. His injured leg outstretched, he held his golden head in his hands, the overlong locks shielding his features, his shoulders heaving silently.

To her surprise, Ian followed him down and placed a familiar hand on Sommerfeld's shoulder. He continued to speak softly, to which Sommerfeld nodded, though he did not lift his head. Ian stood, offered a gentle smile to Juliette and the rest of their audience, and then ducked back into the room. Ethan came to Juliette's side and wrapped an arm around her shoulders.

"Is there anything we can do, Sommerfeld?" Ethan asked softly, treading the fine line between intrusive and friendly. The hallway was stuffed tight with tension. What had happened? Would Lady Sommerfeld be alright?

The viscount finally looked up, turning quickly to the side to swipe at his face. To all their surprise, he emitted a strangled laugh. "My wife is pregnant," he uttered incredulously. "And she will be fine. The baby is moving and seems strong. McCullom explained this happens sometimes, this sort of minor hemorrhage. There is no reason for it." Sommerfeld shook his head disbelievingly. "She needs good food, rest, and peace, but all should be well."

Ethan crouched and held a hand out to the viscount, hauling him to his feet when their hands clasped and hugging him in a strong embrace.

"That is wonderful news," Ethan congratulated him heartily. Sommerfeld clutched him back.

Juliette bit her lower lip, trying not to allow tears of relief and joy to spill over. Lady Morton was not so lucky; she quietly flicked away a few glittering tears.

Instead, Juliette busied herself with retrieving Sommerfeld's cane, intending only to hand it to him and take her leave to allow him privacy; however, Sommerfeld caught her eye before she could escape. He stepped closer to her and accepted his cane.

"Thank you," he began in a low tone to prevent her brother from overhearing too much, though he'd already busied himself with speaking to a passing maid; "for inviting McCullom. Lord knows what would have happened if you hadn't." The viscount squeezed her shoulder in gratitude. "Meredith will need to rest for at least a few weeks before traveling—especially given the distance to my family's estate in Kent. I realize this is an imposition, but might we stay on until she's well enough to move?"

"Certainly!" Juliette replied immediately. "Do not hesitate to let us know if there is anything you require. I want the both of you to be as comfortable as possible."

Sommerfeld inclined his head in gratitude but gently grabbed her elbow when she turned to leave. He dipped his head and spoke in an even lower tone. "I am granting you a small reprieve because I wish to be with my wife now and because I am indebted to you." Juliette's stomach flipped and her cheeks flushed with mortification. "But I am honor-bound to tell you brother what I discovered earlier." His piercing green eyes searched hers as he hesitated before his next question. "He did not force you, did he?"

She reared back. "Of course not!" she hissed.

He nodded, seeming more than a little relieved. "Take a few days to consider the situation. I will allow you to think on how you would like to present it before I bring it to Hopesend's attention. It is not my intention to bring you pain or difficulties, but your brother has been a good friend and he is an honorable man. I cannot in good conscience allow this to continue beneath his roof and pretend I saw nothing. A brother, myself, I would wish to confirm my sister is in good hands."

She averted her eyes in silent acknowledgment and the viscount ducked into the room with his wife and Ian.

*****

It wasn't long before Ian quit the room with his medical bag, leaving George and Meredith alone. George quickly shucked his shirt before climbing into bed with his wife. She looked so small and pale in her white nightshift and clean ivory bed linens. He pulled her close to him with infinite care and cradled her there as she curled into his protective embrace. Together, they simply listened to the sounds of their heartbeats and mingling breaths for a long while without speaking.

"How long have you known about the pregnancy?" George finally asked. There was no accusation in his tone, only curiosity, wonder, and fatigue.

"A few months… I wanted to wait until I was further along before I said something in case the worst happened."

"Then what?" George stiffened. "You would keep it to yourself and grieve alone? You would deny me the opportunity to experience my own grief for our child? For what you had to endure?" He heard her sniff and held her closer, softening his voice once more. This woman had weathered more than many others could have, and she'd done so with a firm hold upon her dignity. To see her bare her soul with such raw candor was both a privilege and terrifying because she held so much inside. "I did not marry you to obtain the ideal of a family, I married you because I love you as you are, regardless of what the future may or may not have in store for us." George's throat thickened.

"There will be no grieving, Meredith. You are healthy and strong. The babe will be well. We will have our family."

She clutched onto him as joy engulfed them both.

"Are you pleased?" she asked in a watery voice.

George tilted his head to gaze down into his wife's indigo eyes. He kissed her deeply and then said, "You always manage to find a way to prove to me that there will always be another pinnacle of happiness, just when I'd thought I'd achieved the greatest possible. I naively believed I'd lived a fulfilling life before my injury, but it is nothing compared to what you have given me. You warm me every day with your presence. And now, you are giving me the greatest gift of all—being the most wonderful mother to my child."

They fell asleep in one another's arms, neither willing to be the first to relinquish the comfort of their hold.

*****

Juliette returned to her rooms to find them cold and empty. She hadn't exactly expected to find Ian waiting there, but a small part of her had hoped. The rational part of her knew it was for the best, given the current circumstances, but that didn't stop the ache in her chest when she found herself alone with hints of him around her.

The sheets were still hopelessly crumpled and they held the scent of their skin and all that had transpired. His coat lay discarded haphazardly on the edge of her desk. But Ian was nowhere to be found. Against her better judgment, she gathered his coat and traversed the darkened hallways by memory alone, not willing to risk a candle with guests and servants still awake and about, until she reached Ian's door.

She debated for a moment whether to knock but decided against it and was pleased to discover it was not locked. She found him shirtless, scrubbing his tools in a steaming basin delivered from the kitchens. So focused on his task was he that he did not immediately register her intrusion. Her eyes drank their fill of the elongated planes of his broad body, the golden light playing across his flesh as the muscles flexed beneath the skin. They had bunched in such a pleasing way as he'd risen above her—God, was it only an hour before? She pressed her fingertips to her temple and the small movement gave her away. His deep blue eyes found hers and he froze. Her pulse began to thrum with awareness, her body oblivious to the fact that this was one of the least opportune moments. They'd been caught in an illicit embrace and Ian had just been forced to examine and treat one of his oldest and dearest friends. The man had to be exhausted, or, at the very least, his mind was as messy and disjointed as hers.

"Lord Sommerfeld was blindingly grateful you were here to help the viscountess in her time of need. I admit I am as well." She twisted her fingers beneath the drape of his coat, still trembling from the myriad emotions roiling inside of her stomach. "I am—"

"Sommerfeld saw us," Ian cut her off gruffly. "There is no possibility of spinning this in any way that might be satisfactory." She watched in silence as he used quick, efficient movements to dry his tools and store them. He threw a clean linen shirt over his head and faced her directly. "I plan to leave in the morning…after I speak to your brother and explain the situation."

"No!" Juliette was nearly choked by her instantaneous panic. To her surprise, it was triggered less by the thought of infuriating her brother than it was by the realization that there would be no possibility of her seeing Ian again. Ever. "Lord Sommerfeld pulled me aside and offered us time. There is no need to make hasty decisions. We have time to—to figure this out—to spin this so it isn't as—"

"Damning? Damaging? How the hell are we supposed to put in a positive light the fact that I've defiled you?" Juliette nearly cringed when he put it so crassly, but she stopped herself. "It is finished, Juliette. Everything is over. You and I both know it will be far worse if your brother does not hear the truth from us first, so we may as well be done with it." He sighed and his eyes became unfocused on a spot over her shoulder. Ian knew his practice would be ruined. He'd be forced to retreat to Scotland to try to gain some footing there and salvage what little reputation he might retain. No doubt Juliette would be married off to the first lord willing to accept damaged goods for a large enough settlement and, if it came to pass, raise any child as his own. The thought nearly made Ian sick right then and there. He hadn't taken any precautions and he damned himself to hell for it.

In being foolish enough to follow Juliette's childish game, they would both now lose everything. Juliette would be forced to relinquish any modicum of freedom she'd managed to wrest from her brother who, in turn, would never trust her again. Ian would lose all he'd worked for and everything his mother had sacrificed would be for naught.

He could read in the shimmering blue of Juliette's eyes how she was struggling against it, but she knew he was right…and it made Ian's soul whither a little more in his breast.

"You don't know Ethan," she said shakily, clutching his coat hands in her hands with a white-knuckled fierceness. "He would never lay a hand upon *me*, but he can have a volatile temper. As even-keeled as he seems, it hides the potential for explosive anger." Ian had heard whispers of the earl's volatility, but it felt more dangerous from Juliette's lips. No one knew him better in the world. "There is no telling what he might do if he discovers someone—you, no less—had defiled his precious sister." Juliette had somehow crossed the space between them without him noticing and reached out to place a hand on his arm. "Please, let us find some other way to approach this together.

There has to be—" She stopped when he took a large step back and out of her reach.

Her sudden stricken expression nearly undid him, but Ian remained as cool as he could manage when he said, "You must leave before anyone else finds us alone together. This ruse has gone on long enough; it is past time for us to part ways as adults and move on. I should have listened to my conscience and avoided this situation like a plague." Though he was the one to say the words, Ian was having a difficult time believing them.

And he knew he would never forget Juliette and the sight of her tear-filled eyes as she turned to leave. It would haunt him to his grave.

God help him.

He'd forever ache for the feel of her in his arms, the scent of her upon his skin, the taste of her, the sound of her melodic voice as she challenged him… Though the last thing he wished to do was admit it to himself, he knew he was going to be leaving an integral part of his heart behind when he left the estate.

The rest of the sleepless night was spent telling himself over and over that Juliette would be fine. She possessed a young, resilient heart. She'd pick herself up, marry a peer, bear his children, and take her rightful place as a respected lady. While he…he wanted nothing more than to crawl into a craggy Highland cave in shame.

Shame for allowing his heart to win over reason and destroy everything he'd fought to accomplish.

Chapter Seventeen

The next morning dawned eerily gray as if Mother Nature had cast a pall upon the house party. Gone was the beautiful weather of the prior days; instead, the clouds hung low and heavy, promising rain. Those guests interested in grouse and hare were off hunting. Ian caught wind that polite excuses had been made for Lord and Lady Sommerfeld and there were whispers that the party might be cut short.

Unable to sleep the night before, Ian had lain awake until he was finally claimed by the arms of a restless unconsciousness, held there until after the hunting and shooting parties had already left for the fields, the earl among them.

He was unsure if it was to his benefit that he now had to wait to speak to the earl until after the hunt was finished. Either the younger man's bloodlust would have been slaked, or his appetite might only have been whetted.

As Ian sipped tea in the breakfast room, his solitary state affording him the freedom to stand at the tall windows to watch the clouds roll in over the hills, he caught a glimpse of deep pink skirts out of the corner of his eye. He recognized Juliette's gait and scent anywhere.

Torn between wanting desperately to speak to her and knowing full well he was better off silent, the decision was made for him when Juliette refused to look him in the eye, let alone acknowledge his presence. It was probably for the best, though that did not stop him from watching her and noting the shadows blemishing the delicate skin beneath her puffy eyes. She appeared as miserable as he felt inside and it ate away at Ian's soul like acid.

He watched from his position by the window as she claimed a chair and proceeded to push her food across her plate, not taking a single bite. After several minutes of this, Ian claimed a seat down the table and across from her, giving her space even though it killed him.

Ian signaled for more tea and the footman ducked from the room to collect a fresh pot. No sooner had the door swung shut than Juliette whispered, "I've fallen in love with you." Ian nearly dropped his fork. His eyes flew to her, but she had not looked up. He might have believed himself mistaken had she not continued to speak. "I know you told me not to, but I couldn't help it when you're so bloody wonderful—when you give me your childhood books, tease me in foreign tongues, and your greatest aspirations are purely selfless. You want nothing more than to bring better medical care to the far-flung corners of the kingdom so no other families will suffer what you have. How could I not fall in love with you, Ian?" Her shoulders heaved with a shaky sigh. "Of course, it is against my better judgment and I've lain awake trying to decide whether or not to say something. But there you have it. The truth is in the open now. You may believe me to be nothing more than a silly girl with fantastical dreams, but I assure you this is no infatuation built upon a few flirtatious glances." She finally met his eyes and what he saw there struck him like a physical blow. She placed her hand to her chest when she spoke again. "I know what is in my heart, and it aches for the brilliant, wonderful man you are."

The pain Ian experienced in his heart was so great that he was forced to close his eyes as her words reverberated through him.

Even sitting this near to her was like a balm to his spirit, hearing those words from her lips was like nothing he'd ever experienced, and he was terrified to admit just how much he savored them. Ian knew deep down, however, that Juliette did not fully realize the implications of what she was saying, of what a life with him would entail, of what she would have to give up if she really did choose him.

Ian took a deep, bracing breath. Just as he opened his mouth to speak, however, the silence was shattered by the barking and baying of hounds outside the window as if they were heralding the arrival of Doomsday.

Ian stood, his heart pounding as the time of reckoning grew nearer. His fingers itched to touch Juliette, but it was not to be.

The earl and his comrades stormed into the house, reeking of horseflesh, gunpowder, and blood, a collective joyful guffaw of death-fueled hormones. Ian risked a glance at Juliette one last time, but it was a grave miscalculation. She read his intentions in his eyes and, just as he began to move, she threw her napkin across her untouched plate of food and made to head him off to the doorway. Unfortunately, despite the difference in the length of their strides, she beat him. Short of tackling her, Ian was forced to allow her to greet her brother first. She stood ahead of him as if to block him—as futile attempt as any he'd ever seen because he was a good head taller than she.

"Ethan!" Juliette said a little too loudly, a squeak to her voice underscoring the anxiety he knew she felt. The earl smiled in greeting, excused himself from his companions. All the men made deferential bows in her direction before carrying their excited chatter down the hallway where refreshments had been laid out in the parlor. He looked every part of the earl with his bright red hunting coat, gold piping and buttons, buff buckskin breeches, and immaculately shined black Hessians. He'd removed his riding gloves and smacked them gently against his opposite palm.

"Good morning, sister." The earl's eyes caught sight of Ian over Juliette's shoulder. Though his ice-blue gaze did not warm, he did incline his head in recognition. Ian bowed stiffly.

"How was the hunt?" Juliette asked, drawing her brother's attention back to her.

"We bagged sacks of game for supper this evening. I expect Cookie will be quite pleased. And what can I do for you, Dr. McCullom?" inquired Hopesend, more interested in why Ian was with his sister than any banal niceties. "Is anything else required for Lady Sommerfeld's care and recuperation?"

"No, but I was hoping I might perhaps request a few minutes of your time, my lord."

The earl's dark brows briefly knit together before he inclined his head and gestured for Ian to follow. Ian inhaled one last deep breath before stepping around Juliette and following Hopesend down the hallway.

Juliette's heart raced like a panicked rabbit as she watched her brother lead Ian across the hallway to his study. Indecision froze her for just a moment before she balled her fists and braced herself to follow, slipping into the room just before her brother could fully shut the door.

Ian shot her a pointed look but said nothing.

Ethan's brow furrowed and he asked if there was something she needed.

Her answer was pathetic, but it was all her frantic mind could produce. "I feel that I should be present for this conversation. I know it concerns me."

Her brother froze in the center of the room, glancing back and forth between Juliette and Ian. The confusion upon his face was made more remarkable by the fact that Juliette didn't think she could recall another time he'd looked just so.

"What is going on?" Ethan's voice was low with foreboding.

"Very well," Ian cleared his throat and began. "First, I would like to thank you for your hospitality this past week." Ethan raised one brow and then the other when Ian continued. "Please accept my sincerest apologies for what I am about to say. You deserve to know the truth of it rather than hearing it second-hand." The pregnant silence was so heavy it made the air in the room difficult to breathe, more so when Ian flicked his eyes at Juliette before looking her brother dead-on when he spoke the next sentence. "Lady Juliette and I shared relations."

Juliette cringed when Ethan's wild eyes flew to her. "What?" he demanded incredulously. "How?" The first sparks of anger began to flare in his eyes as the weight of the admission take root. Instinctively, Juliette stepped forward and opened her mouth to speak, fully prepared to accept the entirety of the blame for the situation, as well as the brunt of her brother's rage. Ian cut her off with a small gesture of his hand at his hip and spoke instead.

"I understand your anger, my lord, and I plan to leave immediately."

"You're damned right you will," Ethan growled. The tremor and wildfire rising to her brother's face served only to underscore Ian's calmness. She knew him well enough to recognize the tightly coiled control in Ian's broad shoulders.

"I care for her…quite deeply, as a matter of fact." Juliette's heart tripped at his words, hope just beginning to blossom in her breast. "I would offer for Lady Juliette's hand if I thought it might make things right—"

"Make it right?" Ethan snarled and went on to confirm exactly what Juliette had feared. "As if I would ever allow her, a lady, to marry you, a Scottish physician with no name and an even less reputable background." Juliette barely resisted placing a hand on Ian's arm when she noticed how tightly his fists were clenched. Her brother's reaction effectively stole any joy she might have felt at Ian's admission that he had feelings for her. "I know exactly the dirt-poor hovel from whence you came, McCullom; you're a fool if you think I would allow anyone around my sister without having first been investigated. It would seem your baser heathen nature could hide itself no longer when faced with such temptation."

"That is unfair, Ethan." Juliette faced her brother squarely, unwilling to allow him to berate Ian further, especially not when she'd been so much at fault for the situation. "You are wounded and lashing out because of it." She froze when Ian's hand closed over her wrist, suffusing her with bolstering warmth and, simultaneously, causing her brother to fly into a rage.

"Ethan, no!" she screeched in shock. In the blink of an eye, her brother charged Ian. She didn't recognize the person grappling with the man she loved, not the bloodthirst in his dark eyes, the crimson tint to his cheeks, the disheveled appearance. She thanked God Ian was taller and broader than her brother because there otherwise would likely have been a murder.

"How dare you lay a hand on her?" Ethan roared, shoving Ian backward. "How dare you take advantage of a woman who is your better? No doubt you saw an easy target with her naïveté."

Ian was holding himself in check, standing his ground when other men would have sprawled on the floor. She didn't know how much longer Ian would be able to do so, however.

A single strong shove nearly sent Ethan sprawling, but he made up for it with his words. He spewed vile curses upon Ian's head, inciting all manner of blasphemy and calling him names which made her ears fairly burn.

As her brother continued to rave, she quickly became aware that their once private conversation had likely drawn quite a bit of attention from the staff and guests. Even if the words couldn't be heard, the shouts and thud of toppled chairs would be unmistakable.

Ethan whirled on Juliette, his eyes unnervingly dark and soulless. "I spent years protecting you and this is how you repay me, sister?" Ethan spoke through gritted teeth. "By sneaking behind my back, undermining me, and effectively destroying all the work I've done in setting you up as a precious jewel of the *ton*?"

"Enough!" Ian's clear, booming voice drew an intangible line between the siblings. Juliette's heart thudded painfully in her chest, but she wasn't afraid; especially not with Ian there. "You did an exemplary job of locking her away from the world, not protecting her," Ian said dangerously as he stepped toe-to-toe with Ethan, taking advantage of his height and added weight. The rolling lilt to his voice deepened as he continued. "And you're foolish to expect anything less from a woman as intelligent as she when you starve her for true life. Juliette has a remarkable mind and a thirst to experience the world. It is nothing but a mark of your youthful hubris that you believed locking someone like your sister away would keep her safe.

"No, it does not excuse what transpired, but maybe it will teach you that all the control in the world would never truly stop someone as determined as she. Accounting for everything but the human spirit is a tragic mistake."

Ethan's jaw worked so hard that Juliette was afraid he might crack all his molars. "Get. Out." Ethan's growl brooked no further conversation. A tense moment passed between them before Ian seemed certain she would be unharmed in his absence, and then he inclined his head and turned to leave.

In his wake, Ethan silently seethed, chest heaving, eyes unfocused on the carpet between them. Never had she witnessed her twin in such a state. She hated his reaction, loathed the things he'd said to Ian, but he was still her beloved brother.

"Ethan," she whispered his name, but there was no indication he'd heard her. "Ethan," she said a little more loudly. "If you will only allow me to explain—" Her words stopped abruptly when he held up a hand to silence her. She bit her lower lip as he rubbed his eyes with his thumb and forefinger, still breathing heavily, but more evenly than before.

"I need to sort this out…to decide what to do with you." He met her eyes and, for the first time since this horrible encounter had begun, she saw something else there. Pain. Betrayal. And she knew he would never look at her again as he used to. An irreparable alteration had been made to their bond. A twinge of guilt began to build behind her sternum, but she refused to cave into it. Juliette was past thinking about how her behavior might be viewed by her brother. She was many years beyond the point where she was a shy sapling of a girl, bending to every gusty blow of whim and influence from the small bubble around her. Ian had shown her that there was so much more to the world, life, to *her* than she had ever believed possible.

Ethan broke their gaze and rushed past her, the dust from his riding boots trailing in his wake as he bellowed for his gloves and crop, for his horse to be brought back 'round from the stables.

Several guests had been milling about outside the office and, while it had been easy for Ethan to blow past them, several curious eyes peered into the study to stare aghast at her. None approached her.

Her cheeks burned, but not for herself…for the fact that Ian had been forced to traverse this wicked garden of leering gazes on his own.

Juliette left standing alone in the study to wonder at the mess she'd made was nothing in comparison to the disaster she had visited upon Ian.

Chapter Eighteen

An hour later, a carriage had been made ready and Ian's trunks were stacked and strapped to it one by one. He managed the task as he did most everything else in his life—quick efficiency and methodical order.

He had no desire to encounter Hopesend again before he took his leave, so he did his best to keep to his corner of the house and only ventured forth when it was time, once more, to check on Meredith. Her bright red hair had been plaited and she rested comfortably in the large bed. Color had returned to her cheeks and her eyes misted over with grateful tears when Ian repeatedly reassured her that the bleeding had stopped and all indications pointed to a healthy pregnancy so long as she rested and continued to eat the prescribed diet rich in the sustenance her body required. She clutched his hand and, where he'd once felt a powerful rush of desire, there was only a deep-rooted affection. His heart would always lean toward his longtime friend, but it now belonged steadfastly in the delicate hands of another.

When he was finished, Sommerfeld followed Ian out into the adjacent sitting room, closing the door behind him. Ian needed less than a moment to discern what was coming next, so he headed it off.

"I don't doubt you heard of this morning's incident." The viscount had enough grace to avert his eyes. "It went about as poorly as can be expected," explained and turned his gaze to the pastoral scene outside the window. He was startled back into himself by Sommerfeld's hand on his shoulder. Ian's eyes flicked from the gesture and into the viscount's green eyes.

"Condolences." He removed his hand with an awkward gesture. "I've been well acquainted with the earl for several years now. I don't know how successful I will be, but I can attempt to smooth things over with him once you take your leave." Whether out of pity or gratitude for how Ian had helped both him and Meredith, regardless, Sommerfeld seemed genuinely sincere in his offer. If those words had been a surprise, the next were a shock.

"I am man enough to admit that I haven't always treated you fairly, Dr. McCullom," Sommerfeld said in a low voice. "And I may not be proud of it, but I have experienced jealousy once or twice when it comes to your history with my wife. But, I can admit that I am certain you are not someone who takes advantage of anyone. I've never known you to be a man anything other than professional and proper. If this…situation with Lady Juliette transpired as I suspect it did, then Lady Juliette went into it with her eyes wide open. You never would have used her. And I believe she must also mean a great deal to you if you were willing to risk so much for her." Sommerfeld cast a glance over his shoulder where his wife lay in the bed beyond the door, silently conveying he understood and would do the same—risk everything for the woman who owned his heart.

At a loss for any proper words, Ian could only incline his head in gratitude. The viscount offered him a handclasp, which Ian accepted gratefully.

Just as Ian was supervising the loading of the last of his items, there was a commotion from the house. Ian paused with one hand on the carriage door, poised to hoist himself aloft, when Juliette burst from the front door to form a tableau Ian would never forget as long as he lived.

The bodice of her morning dress was stained scarlet, it coated her palms and smeared up her bare arms, a smudge of it marred the perfect flesh of her cheek. His name being torn from her lips set him into immediate motion. Lunging toward her, Ian immediately ran his hands over her body, trying to locate the source of the bleeding.

"Where are you hurt?" he demanded, doing his best to ignore the unsteadiness of his hands, the quake in his voice, the painful thumping of his heart, the ringing in his ears. "What did he do?"

Her bright, frantic eyes met his and she shook her head. "Not me," she gasped. "Not me."

"What happened?"

"There was an accident," Juliette stammered.

Ian's hands gripped her more tightly. "Show me," he said more steadily before now that he knew she was not the injured party. Knowing Juliette was safe allowed Ian's pulse to slow as he slid into his physician's persona.

Ian shed his coat as they dashed to the back of the house and down to the kitchens. The earl's valet met them an rapidly explained how Hopesend had taken off on his horse once more following their earlier confrontation. He'd been furious and reckless. Recognizing the danger, a couple of the other male guests who had taken part in the hunt returned to their mounts and followed shortly behind to try to calm him. They had caught up to the earl just in time to see the horse—already on edge from its furious rider—shying as a hare dated across the way. The animal had balked violently, but the earl would have been able to keep his seat had the horse not fallen. He had landed beneath the beast, striking his head on a rock.

Hopesend had been carried back to the house, bleeding and unconscious, and was now lying on the long wooden table in the kitchens. The staff had been shooed out, their various tasks left unfinished and scattered around them like detritus following an explosion.

His assessing gaze traveled the length of the earl's unconscious form, noting the dirt and blood, the awkward angle of his left arm.

"Retrieve my leather satchel from inside the carriage," Ian barked at the nearest pale-faced footman. The lad appeared almost grateful for the task, at being allowed to leave the room filling with the metallic stench of blood and sweat. The men with stronger stomachs would be needed for what Ian must do.

Juliette watched with numb amazement as Ian examined her brother. Refusing to be ushered from the room, she made herself as unobtrusive as possible and held Ethan's gloved hand in her own. He was so pale, so mortal. His dark curls were plastered to his head, matted with mud and twigs, and blood so dark it didn't appear real.

In addition to his broken arm, that shoulder was badly dislocated and the cut inflicted by the rock on the side of his head ran jaggedly from his left temple back through his hairline.

Though her brother's care absorbed Ian's attention, Ian must have seen the color drain from her face because he still did his best to reassure her. "Even superficial headwounds bleed profusely." He moved to the hearth where a pot bubbled away with water and dropped his metal instruments into it.

Quickly, her brother's clothing was cut from his body until he was bare from the waist up to reveal the lean length of his torso. Ian proceeded to scrub his hands with hot water and the clean-scented cake of soap he carried in his medical bag. He moved around the room with grace and poise, deftly instructing two strong footmen to help him set Ethan's shoulder with brute force.

The loud pop that followed made Juliette nauseous, but she refused to leave even when she felt the burn of Ian's eyes upon her. She knew he hadn't liked it when she'd refused to abandon her post before the procedure. Though Ian had given her an out, suggesting she wash up and he would retrieve her when he was done, she'd refused and he had allowed her to remain where she was. More than her brother, Ethan was her twin. She hurt when he did. And if the worst happened…she would lose a part of herself as integral as an eye or a limb. She wouldn't know how to function without Ethan, so she simply had to stay.

Ian proceeded to clean Ethan's head wound after setting and splinting the arm and fashioning a sling. She watched in morbid fascination as Ian, using a sterilized needle and silk thread, closed the gash in her brother's temple with stitches so fine they would put many young ladies to shame. A poultice was then applied, followed by a bandage wound around his head. Ian murmured to her as he worked, telling her that he hadn't felt any cracks in the skull, so her brother's recovery depended upon whether or not there was swelling of the brain. The next day or two would be integral. Though she and Ian didn't touch or speak with one another much, they worked together to oversee Ethan's transfer from the kitchens to his private rooms and the changing of his clothing as he was settled into his bed.

"I have something I can give him for pain, but we must refrain from drugging him too much," Ian said softly, evenly when they were alone with Ethan's still form. He looked so young, so pale nestled among the pillows and deep blue coverlet. "We need him to regain consciousness, not sleep more deeply."

Juliette smoothed Ethan's freshly washed blue-black hair back until she encountered the stark whiteness of the bandage Ian had so skillfully wound around his head.

"Thank you," she whispered, her voice hoarse from emotion and disuse. "Thank you, Ian."

A heavy silence stretched out between them until Ian finally spoke once more. "His lordship likely won't care for it, but I can stay on until he wakes—"

"Stay." Juliette tempered her next words when she realized how abrupt her outburst had sounded. "Please, stay." She met his eyes and her entire body began to ache from fatigue and the onslaught of emotions that had been churning within her throughout that day. "I would not want anyone else treating him."

She noticed a twitch of a muscle in Ian's jaw before he inclined his head and replied, "As you wish." He then excused himself to tidy the mess in the kitchens and clean his utensils, leaving Juliette to turn back to her brother and clasp his hand in both of hers.

Chapter Nineteen

Two Months Later

The Fall air was crisp and clear as Ian walked through the streets of Edinburough toward the comfortable home he'd purchased for his mother the year before. It wasn't an enormous house, but it was sturdy and sound, and she never again had to worry about a fickle landlord.

Ever a woman who wanted to stay busy, Margaret McCullom continued to bake for local households, selling her sweets and meat pies to the maids and cooks she'd come to know throughout her years of service. She'd taken the money she earned and used it to turn the four walls Ian had purchased for her into a home. At least once each week, she would stand in that home and turn in circles, marveling at the fact that her son had provided so well for her—how lucky she was that he loved her as he did. And it brought tears to her eyes every single time. Nothing gave her as much joy, however, as having her son home with her.

Ian had never disclosed his reason for the visit from London, nor how long he planned to stay, only walked through the door, kissed her on the cheek, and stole a morsel from her chopping board like when he'd been a wee lad. He'd promptly unpacked his things in the spare bedroom without a word. Margaret had been considering letting out one of those rooms to a young lady in town so she wouldn't have to walk so far to work before sunrise, but that could wait until Ian returned to London; he was never able to stay for very long.

In the weeks since his arrival, Ian had remained steadfastly evasive to all her questions. He'd always been a boy of few words—she liked to say he saved them for when they really counted—but it was irksome to a mother who knew when some. Regardless of the reason behind it, she was pleased to have him home; she loved showing him off as her pride and joy.

Each time someone came to pick up an order of her baking, she would make a big show of explaining how her son, the physician, was in town and loved a particular treat, and she'd introduce him as such to anyone who would listen.

One time, she'd commented to him that perhaps he'd like to settle down soon—maybe move back to Edinburough to be near to her when bairns came. He'd only given her a sidelong look and picked up his book.

That day, as Ian was walking the winding city streets of New Town, there was a knock at the door. At first, Margaret was confused—there weren't any scheduled pick-ups the rest of the day. She set aside her knife, wiped her hands on her apron, and answered the door to find a very beautiful, very exhausted-looking young woman. Her thick, blue-black hair was pulled back beneath a fashionable raspberry-pink hat affixed with gold-tipped pins. She wore a matching traveling gown fitted to her arms with impeccable tailoring, a modest neckline trimmed in pink lace, and thick velvet skirts falling in graceful panels. Her eyes were wide, and remarkably dark and intelligent.

"Aye?"

"Is this the McCullom residence?" the woman asked, not bothering to mask the hopeful note to her voice. *Sasannach*. And a wealthy one by the looks of her clothing. Margaret had worked in enough households and served enough nobility to know quality when she saw it.

"Aye." She gripped the door a little tighter, wondering at this woman's intentions, especially when she hesitated before her next question.

"Are you Mrs. McCullom? Mother to Dr. Ian McCullom?"

She nodded in reply, curious if this woman was a patient of his and how she'd come to find their home, but the young woman's face lit up in delight, turning her beautiful face incandescent.

"I am so very pleased to meet you! I am a friend of Ian—Dr. McCullom. Is he in?"

Margaret frowned. "Nay. He's out and, knowing him, he won't return for several hours. He's a very busy mon." The Englishwoman was immediately crestfallen and Margaret was suddenly overcome by the urge to comfort her. Something about the candor in her eyes, she supposed. She was unable to turn the girl away. "Ye sound like you've traveled a long way. Would ye like to come in and set awhile? Eat a bite?" She stepped to the side and the woman thanked her graciously as she entered the home that smelled warmly of herbs and buttery shortbread.

Ian stomped up the front steps of his mother's home more exhausted from his errands than if he'd set two legs, sewn a dozen lacerations, treated a handful of croupy dowagers, and assisted in the birth of three babes. What he wouldn't have given for those days…

Instead, he'd spent his time scouting for a new office space and sending messages to his solicitor in London to begin the process of liquidating his London practice. It had been a rather depressing, fruitless day.

Needing some cheer, he'd passed through a market on the way and, while most of the stalls had been closed or picked over, he managed to snag a few good apples and a respectable bouquet of flowers. Arms full, he used the heel of his boot to close the door when he was inside.

"*Mama?*" he called, juggling his purchases. "*Tha fàileadh blasta.*" *It smells delicious.* The house was filled with the sweet scent of pastries and the rich, nutty aroma of browned butter. His stomach gave an involuntary growl. "*Bidh mi reamhar ma dh'fhuiricheas mi an seo fada nas fhaide.*" *I will become fat if I stay here much longer.* And he would; already his clothing was becoming a touch snug from the consistent, rich, comforting meals only a mother could provide.

Ian stepped into the kitchen and his every muscle froze. The apples nearly tumbled from his arm, but he managed to rescue them just in time.

His mother was beaming so much that the glitter in her dark chocolate eyes was nearly blinding. Her plump cheeks were flushed from equal measures of joy and the heat of the close room.

"*Tha Gàidhlig na h-Alba aig a' chaileag seo, an robh fios agad?*" she tittered like a girl. *This girl speaks Gaelic, did you know?* "*Tha i math gu leòr airson Sasannach!*" *She is quite good for an English-woman!*

Ian was still struck dumb with disbelief, staring at Juliette as she stood elbow-deep in powdery flour, helping his mother finish some dough for their supper.

"*Tha i gòrach air bèicearachd, ach chan e rud beag a th' ann nach socraich cleachdadh.*"

"*Mama!*" Ian gasped, his face growing uncomfortably warm as he hoped Juliette hadn't been able to translate the words: *She is shite at baking, but it is nothing a little practice won't fix.* Unfortunately, a small, amused smile on Juliette's full lips told Ian he had no such luck. He wanted to apologize for his mother's blunt comment, but his brain struggled to process the domestic sight before him.

Surely his body was lying dead in the street somewhere, because this could not possibly be real.

He watched in fascination as Juliette wiped her hands on her deep pink skirts, likely ruining them, but not caring one whit. His heart stuttered when her eyes met his.

"Hello, Ian," she said softly, carefully, as if unsure of the reception. How could she not know how every inch of his skin screamed for her, that he was bruising the fragile apples and flower stems in his hands in an effort not to reach for her?

"What are you doing here?" he croaked. How many nights had he lain awake with his heart too heavy to sleep, his arms unbearably empty, his entire being aching for her, mind, body, heart, and soul?

"Ian!" came his mother's warning voice; it was apparently her turn to remind him of his manners. "*Bi spèis,*" she snapped. *Be respectful.*

Juliette's head inclined to mask a coy smile. She'd somehow been practicing her Gaelic in the interminable weeks since they'd last seen one another.

Ian set down his burdens and he and Juliette eyed one another from across the flour-covered table. The weeks of absence and unspoken words simmered in the air between them.

His mother's eyes darted between them. "It seems ye two have some talking to do," she said in her rough-hewn English. "I'll finish in here; you go to the other room and say what needs to be said without *Mama* in the way. Leave supper to me."

Juliette flashed a smile of gratitude and led the way from the kitchen. They found their way to the back room Ian had commandeered for his study. It was close and warm with barely enough space to walk around the trunks, small desk, and chair pressed tightly against the walls, but it was far enough away that his mother would have difficulty overhearing them. Both of them refused to sit in the single chair.

Ian cleared his throat. "How fares your brother?" The question was one of the last on his mind, but it was the most polite and least difficult one to ask.

"Well enough to begin barking orders," Juliette replied with a little laugh through her nose. "He seems less upset about his injuries than the fact that the hunting party had to be cut short because of the accident and Lady Sommerfeld's condition. It has been dubbed 'The Cursed Party.'"

"And how is Lady Sommerfeld?" The stilted formalities were killing him slowly, but it was all he trusted himself to do.

"The viscount grows restless to bring her to Bridleton, but he is afraid to move her too soon. My brother and I have made it very clear to them both that they are welcome to stay as long as they need to."

This last was followed by a prolonged silence.

"Are you going to inquire as to my health?" Juliette ventured. "You have done so for nearly every one of our other mutual acquaintances thus far."

His mouth tilted in amusement; he couldn't help it. "And you, Lady Juliette? How do you fare?"

"Miserable." Her blunt response with its flat affect nearly knocked him backward. "I have been nothing short of utterly miserable, Ian. I have missed you terribly. I thought this time apart might heal the wound left behind, but it seems to have only made things worse."

Ian's heartbeat increased as she continued. "This is why, as soon as I could be certain my brother was well on his way to recovery, but would not yet be well enough to follow through with his threats to keep an even closer eye on me, I fled."

Ian experienced the most curious sensation as simultaneously, his stomach plummeted and his heart soared.

"You fled?" he questioned the obvious—for how else could she be standing there before him if she hadn't escaped her brother?

She nodded. "Allowing you to slip away and hide here in Scotland would have been too easy for you."

"It sounds as if Meredith planted that seed," he said, shaking his head incredulously. "You must know this is a terrible idea, Juliette; you must return home before anyone knows where you have gone."

"Ethan will have found my letter by now, so returning would be useless."

"A note?"

"Isn't it the done thing to leave a note when one runs off to elope?"

"Elope?"

"My, but I did not realize you made such an excellent parrot, Dr. McCullom." Ian's mouth snapped shut at her amused comment. "I love you, Ian," she continued more soberly. "And I know you don't find the prospect of marriage to me abhorrent in the least. I know you care about me; I see it in the way you watch me when you think I am not paying attention, how you are so thoughtful, and how you gift me with your cherished childhood possessions." She pulled his small book from a deep pocket in her skirts and held it out to him. The sight of the battered cover made his chest throb. "Or have I read you incorrectly?"

"You know I want you," he began roughly; "but we simply are not meant to be. You were born to be someone's gently bred wife, not the partner of a man who works long hours for a living. Fate never would have started us on such different paths if our lives were ever meant to intersect."

"Why can I not decide one thing for myself?" Juliette demanded. "All my life, I have been groomed and sheltered, but I knew all the while something was missing. You showed me what it meant to have meaning in one's life. Real meaning. Is it really so bad if I decide *you* are *my* destiny?" Ian's arm darted out and he pulled her roughly to him, but she continued to speak as her powdery hands curled in his lapels. "I want to help you realize your dreams. I want to travel with you as you make the world a better place. We'll go to the Continent where you learned your techniques. We will live in foreign lands and put our linguistic skills to the test."

Heart racing, Ian knew he had to temper her excitement. "Your life would be very different than the one to which you have grown accustomed; your brother may never forgive you or welcome you home with open arms again."

There was a flicker of pain in her eyes which told him she'd considered all of this and had weighed her choice with no little amount of effort. "Despite what you say, I know you are no pauper; I trust with my whole heart that you will provide a safe, comfortable life for both of us. I will be home wherever you are, whether it be Scotland, London, or Constantinople.

"As for Ethan...he will undoubtedly be furious with me, but I do not doubt in my heart that he will eventually forgive me. We are two halves of the same whole; neither can live too long without the other. Besides, I expect he will come to terms with the fact that a happy sister is far preferable to a miserable one beneath his thumb." Juliette's hand slid up Ian's chest, past his cravat, and the pad of her thumb traced the line of his jaw and then the curve of his lower lip, igniting a heat deep within his loins. "*Tha gaol agam ort,*" she whispered in Gaelic, thrilling him beyond reason. *I love you.* "And," she added in English; "I have taken the choice out of your hands. If my reputation hadn't been tattered before, it is well and truly obliterated now. You have no choice but to make things right, do the honorable thing, and keep me as yours forever."

His heart incredibly light in his chest, Ian finally bowed his head to capture Juliette's mouth with his. Their lips and teeth and tongue met with furious need built up over the past several weeks.

"What have I ever done to deserve you," Ian murmured against her lips.

Breath unsteady, she pressed her forehead to his. "Consider it a reward for all the lives you have saved, and have yet to save."

Ian threw back his head and laughed before kissing her once again. He easily swept her slight frame up into his arms and quit the room to head for the stairs. However, their progress was stopped quite abruptly by the sight of Ian's mother blocking their way, hands on her hips, a stern tilt to her mouth, though her eyes twinkling with barely contained joy.

"Now, it's all well and fine that you're planning on gettin' married, but you'll not be doing anything untoward beneath ma roof." She eyed her son. "No matter how old Ian is, I am still his mother. You can wait a couple of days until we're able tuh have a proper ceremony. As me only son, you at least owe me a wedding." Ian felt Juliette's arms tighten around his neck. "Ye don't need to wait for the banns to be read in Scotland, but ye need to postpone everything 'til after Sunday."

Ian emitted an uncharacteristically pained groan; the woman in his arms laughed melodiously and rubbed a conciliatory hand on his chest.

Chapter Twenty

Ian's mother, while a kind, warm woman, turned out to be not very trusting of her son's ability to curb his baser urges. Though Ian had offered to sleep in his office so Juliette could take over his room, Juliette was, instead, deposited at the home of one of Margaret's many friends until the wedding could take place.

Determined that their union be as respectable as possible in the eyes of the English, Ian went to the trouble of procuring a license and calling in favors to make the event as much like a traditional wedding as possible. Juliette had dubbed their situation an elopement, but she deserved so much more than a hasty wedding, no matter how his body yearned to be with her once more. He took great pleasure in procuring a well-appointed suite for them at a hotel in New Town for their honeymoon period where they could have all the time and privacy they desired. From there, travel was arranged to take them to the Continent. The trip he was planning was nearly as exciting as the wedding itself. He could not wait to open up the world to his beloved, to expose her to new and exciting things of which she'd only read, and to show her some of his favorite places. He wanted to experience these things through her eyes and savor them with her. He wanted to make new memories and build a future.

Meanwhile, Margaret took Juliette to purchase a ready-made gown from a modiste on Princes Street. The shopkeeper was flustered when Ian's mother let slip that Juliette was the sister of an earl and there would be no time to design or alter a gown befitting her station. The time constraints of their short engagement meant there were only three dresses from which to choose where alterations could be made in a day.

The first was virginal ivory, but it had far too many frills and made Juliette feel like a young girl. The last thing she wanted was to look like a child's doll on her wedding day. The next was better, but the neckline of the sapphire blue gown was too high. The third, the shop-keeper told her, was an abandoned order where the lady had changed her mind about the color. It was a nearly finished satin gown in the richest green Juliette had ever seen. Lighter green rosettes decorated the cap sleeves which fell just below her natural shoulder to lend a hint of daring; the neckline was trimmed in deep green lace; the waist would be cinched in with a beaded ribbon once it was finished. The hem was a tad too long and the waist an inch too large, but nothing that couldn't be fixed with relative ease and skill. As Juliette examined herself in the looking glass, smoothing the skirts and touching the rosettes, a choked sob hiccuped from behind her.

Ian's mother watched her, hands clasped before her face in a futile attempt to staunch her tears. "Ach," she snuffled. *"Cho breagha…"*

Juliette smiled and held out her hand. The older woman took it and squeezed it in her own weathered, callused one. "Thank you, *Mama*; I certainly feel beautiful." It was difficult to not allow herself to grow emotional as well when faced with this immensely strong woman's joy, but she somehow managed.

Measurements were made, alterations were agreed upon, and Juliette purchased the dress with a small portion of the funds she'd brought on her journey. Juliette took great satisfaction knowing this task brought her one step closer to being with Ian forever.

The day of the wedding dawned bright and sunny. Though the morning chill had yet to burn off by the time the small gathering arrived at the church, Ian still felt as if it was the perfect day to marry a woman far too good for him.

His mother had spent the prior evening alternating between crying, telling him how overjoyed she was that he'd found a life partner, reminding him that the lively gel would keep him on his toes; how she believed the two of them to be perfect counterbalances to one another. This, his mother believed, was the key to all successful marriages: Balance.

She believed Juliette would lighten Ian's seriousness; he, in turn, would ground her. His parents had had a marriage of balance, and Ian looked forward to discovering that sweet point of equality where he and Juliette were partners working in tandem for a singular future.

The ceremony, itself, was traditionally Scottish. The church was decorated with little sprays of native flowers—Scots bluebells, thorny thistles, and heather. The air was filled with the ghosts of Ian's childhood memories, thick with where he'd come from and all he had yet to achieve. It struck him so ferociously that he had to stop a moment, close his eyes, and simply breathe it in. And, when he opened them again, an angel draped in the green earth of the Highlands was floating toward where he stood at the end of the aisle. Words could not describe how beautiful Juliette was to him. Her black hair was plaited and pinned to her head and only when she was closer could he see the little bluebells woven in the delicate strands. Swathed in green silk, draped in a swath of the navy blue, hunter green, black, and gray plaid of his family's ancient clan, she was the softer, more perfect, more feminine version of his attire. He, too, was carried a length of the dyed wool plaid; the very same one his father had worn on his wedding day, and it felt as if a part of him was there beside Ian.

The light filtering through the high, narrow windows caught on the silver brooch at Juliette's shoulder where it held the two halves of her plaid together. It was the same brooch his da' had given to his mother the day before their wedding. It was simple but dearly cherished. When he had watched as Juliette teared up after his mother had given it to her and explained its significance, he could have carried her off and married her right then and there for being so accepting of his heritage, of his past, of his family. This woman took him as he was, wanted him to be nothing more than he was, and loved him for it all. It was blindingly baffling to Ian, but he vowed to accept it, cherish it, nurture it, and return it to Juliette tenfold. Everything about that day was simple and perfect, but it was the love in Juliette's eyes that was truly stunning.

Together, they recited their promises and he slid a thin gold band of interwoven threads onto her finger. When they kissed, Juliette threw her arms around Ian's neck with such enthusiasm that she nearly knocked him from his feet. A few chuckles and a smattering of embarrassed coughs bubbled up from the guests present—mainly Margaret's closest friends—but it was of no consequence; especially when he held his wife's face in his hands, pressed his forehead to hers, and told her he loved her in as many languages as he could think of.

*****

The hastiness of the nuptials meant there hadn't been time to plan a proper wedding breakfast, though his mother had certainly tried to convince them otherwise. Neither Juliette nor Ian minded, though, because they were better able to take their leave more quickly after accepting the well-wishes of the small number of those gathered to celebrate. The moment it was remotely respectable, Ian quickly ushered her into a carriage and they were whisked away to a lavish hotel in New Town.

Aside from the occasional coaching inn, Juliette had never stepped foot inside a hotel—had never traveled far enough from family or friends to require it—but this one far exceeded any expectations she might have had. Hotels in London were beginning to gain notoriety for the luxury and extravagance they afforded; as she looked around at the polished wood and glittering gilt trim, the glowing chandeliers and the immaculately-dressed staff, she had to believe this one could compete with whatever England offered. Surely a room at this hotel would come at no small cost. She nibbled her lip and tried to guess at just how much a night might set one back, but she had no point of reference from which to draw. The last thing she wanted was for Ian to spread himself too thin trying to provide her with the things he believed she wanted or needed. All she needed was him.

They were shown to their room and all of her worries were forgotten the moment Ian swept her in his arms and slung her over his shoulder.

"Ian!" she attempted indignation, but could only manage breathless laughter as he carried her to the oversized bed like a heathen warlord.

"Now, I can finally do what I've wanted to since you showed up in my mother's home, covered yourself in flour, and charmed her with your linguistic skills." He landed a playful swat to her bottom before gently depositing her atop the thick mattress. Standing above her, legs wide and fists at his hips, Juliette's heart began to race and her stomach flipped in anticipation as she examined her husband. *Her husband.* They could be together without fear or shame. They could explore and share and learn together. Pulse pounding, skin tingling with desire and awareness, she opened her arms to Ian and invited him to lie with her. Together at last, they took their time savoring one another, relearning each other's body and how to both give and take their pleasure.

Ian's accent thickened as she neared a shattering release; the words wove around them like an intimate cocoon, as tangible to her as his hands and his teeth and his tongue. Long after they'd both found their release, she closed her eyes and sank into the memory of his rough voice.

"What are you thinking, my love?" Ian asked, his words still slightly breathless with the airiness of satiation.

"How much I enjoy the way your diction loses all its crispness when we lie together." She opened her eyes and grinned at him. "I quite like it."

Ian shot her a wolfish grin and rolled atop her, pinning her arms over her head, stealing her breath with the sudden excitement of it all. "And would ye like to be ravished by an animal rather than a mon, lass? I dinna think yer wee body could take it." His words were thick with an exaggerated accent, bordering on satirical. She couldn't help it, she laughed until she felt his body shaking mirthfully above hers and he pressed a kiss to her exposed throat. He rolled and carried her with him, nestling her against his side within the crook of his arm. And Juliette felt safe, cherished, respected. She couldn't have dreamt of more.

Ian shifted again and placed his large palm upon her chest, just above the beat of her heart. "*Bidh thu a 'cumail mo chridhe agus bidh an-còmhnaidh*," he whispered and Juliette held her breath to catch and clutch his every word. "*Thug an dàn sinn còmhla agus fuirichidh sinn còmhla.*"

Despite her efforts, she could only translate a handful of the words he'd spoken and she was forced to concede. "It's lovely; what does it mean?"

There was a thoughtful moment before Ian replied.

"It means, you hold my heart and always will. Fate brought us together and together we will stay."

Epilogue

Juliette and Ian's honeymoon trip abroad lasted longer than planned. Every new country they visited and each city in which they stopped opened Juliette's eyes to brilliant, amazing things she had never thought to experience.

They started in France and then went through Spain and Portugal before settling in for a longer stay in Italy. At once, Juliette had fallen in love with the culture, and Ian had fallen more in love with her each day.

Somehow, Juliette had easily charmed every last one of Ian's staid and stuffy Italian mentors. Her mastery of their language endeared her to everyone she met and she felt immediately at home in the land of her mother's ancestors. To Ian, she looked as if she belonged. She certainly fit in well with her thick dark hair and innate elegance, but there was more to it than only her appearance. She bloomed beneath the Italian sun and her personality soared amongst the circles of society there. She could speak to anyone young or old, rich or poor, and treated them all with the same care and respect. It was difficult not to fall for her. He'd lost count of all the times Italian men swore never to love another after looking upon Juliette's face or hearing her voice. Despite this, not once did Ian doubt that Juliette would always send those men away with a kind smile and conciliatory word before returning to his side.

She reveled in every experience he showed her. They explored markets and tried new foods. They took in sights of great historical importance and traveled through Venice and Rome. They discussed medical practices and she proved to be a particularly adept partner off whom to bounce ideas for their future together, and that of his career. She impressed him with her earnest desire to do whatever she could to help see his dream through. She was the one who organized his supplies lists for him and, once she'd done that, offered to use her contacts to try to obtain donations and better prices on the items he would need. At the very least, she was positive she could ask Lady Morton to use her Reading Society to help raise funds for Ian's venture. The depth of her heart seemed fathomless, and she affirmed his choice in her over and over again.

Eventually, the call for England became too great. Weeks later than planned, they returned to drizzly shores and were greeted by the great white chalk cliffs of Dover. They did, however, bring one thing home with them from Italy: an apprentice for Ian.

Dottor Lorenzo Bianchi was a promising young man who had come highly recommended by Ian's former mentors. After several meetings with the tall, dark-haired Italian, both Ian and Juliette concluded that Dr. Bianchi would be an excellent asset. After some negotiations, it was decided that he would return with them to England to join Ian's business as an assistant and then a fellow physician. This would, of course, include some additional training and English lessons. This meant Ian would one day have more time to travel and realize his dream of providing quality medical care to more than just the elite.

As Juliette stood on the ship's deck and watched England's shoreline grow ever larger, Ian took her hand in his. He knew the root of the anxiety she tried so hard to mask behind a tremulous smile: They were quite uncertain as to what would greet them when they finally returned to London.

Immediately following their wedding, Ian had instructed his solicitor to hold off on liquidating his London practice until they knew first-hand the fallout of their elopement. He still had to be able to provide a future for Juliette if she wished to remain in England, and the best way for him to do that was to continue catering to the *ton*'s medical needs. His life was about more than just his own goals now; he had to account for her as well. And he would do all that was within his power to give her anything and everything he could.

Ian knew Meredith had written to Juliette a handful of times in the past several months. She always managed to avoid answering Juliette's inquiries about Hopesend's reaction to their elopement, while tactfully requesting confirmation that Ian would be present to assist at the birth of her child. Ever the true friend, though, Meredith always did her best to reassure them that she didn't want them to rush home from their adventures.

He could tell that Meredith's careful omissions increased Juliette's anxieties, but she never failed to impress him with how selfless she could be. His wife confirmed with him at least once each week that they would be able to return to England in time for Meredith's labor; the only person who wanted him there more was Meredith, herself. He and Juliette had shared a lengthy discussion about Ian's previous proposal to his longtime friend. In the end, Juliette had been content with his explanation that he'd *believed* himself in love with Meredith but he *knew* with every fiber of his being that he was in love with Juliette. It was a different love, entirely.

After depositing Dr. Bianchi at the rooms that had been rented for him, Ian and Juliette finally found themselves alone in the foyer of the Townhouse which served as both his office and living quarters. Ian silently mused at how similar the scene was to the day of their first meeting months ago, and the incredible whirlwind that had transpired in between.

He began by guiding her through the rooms on the main floor: spaces typically designated for a sitting room, a small dining room, and one that might be used as a study or library if the pitiable amount of non-medical books in residence could be bolstered. The first floor contained two of the bedchambers, including his own. The uppermost floor held two additional rooms, but Ian hadn't set foot in them since he purchased the property. He could tell instantly that Juliette was stunned by the sparseness of his living conditions. He'd always lived simply and, since he spent so little time there, he hadn't sought fit to place too much emphasis upon making this house into a home.

"We can rent out these rooms and find a new home for us if you would prefer," Ian offered as Juliette wandered through the bedchamber. Much to his surprise, she shook her head.

"I like knowing where to find you if you work late into the night." Her shy smile warmed his heart more than he would have believed possible. "I have only to add my touches to the lovely bones of this house and I believe we will be quite comfortable here."

While Mrs. Brown had kept the house immaculate in his absence, the pile of Ian's correspondence was enormous, spilling off his desk and onto the floor. Outdated invitations, letters, notices, journals, papers...all of it was piled high in as neat of stacks as she had been able to manage. In addition, a running list of names had been kept of all those who had stopped by Ian's office and, per his instructions, they'd been directed to another physician in his absence. It was an unbelievable amount of work and Juliette didn't care for the idea of Ian having to slog through it all on his own.

"May I help you sort through all of this? Please tell me how I can be useful." She stooped to retrieve a few thick envelopes which had tumbled to the floor.

"Thank you, but no," he declined her offer with a lingering kiss. "You have already helped me more than you know. I fear this mess must be organized in an insane only my twisted brain can comprehend." Having seen the chaos of his office before, she fully appreciated the statement. "Why don't you settle in as best you can and start compiling a list of everything we lack here? We can make some purchases and turn this mausoleum of bachelorhood into a home, hm?"

Juliette agreed, but only after wringing a promise from him that he would not stay up too late because she would require his assistance undoing her stays. The infinite pools of Ian's irises darkened appreciatively and she knew he would do exactly as he promised.

Over the next several days, Juliette busied herself with unpacking what little she'd brought with her, getting to know Mrs. Brown—if the formidable woman who'd once barred her from Ian's door thought it odd to find Juliette as her new mistress, she said not a word about it —and she did, indeed, take Ian's suggestion and make a list of items they required. She tried to remain conscientious of the fact that her husband worked for their money, so she ranked the items in order of importance. Somewhere to sit and eat supper, for example, was a higher priority than draperies in the unused bedchambers. She postponed less important purchases in favor of splurges on a new bed, mattress, and quality linens—the absolute essentials for newlyweds who spent as much time as they did in bed. Ian certainly hadn't complained about *those* purchases. Now and again, she would grow wistful about all the books and favorite gowns she'd been forced to leave behind when she fled to Scotland, but then she had only to look at her husband to be reminded of how it had all been worth it. Ian meant so much more to her than piles of gold and unnecessary luxuries.

Ian was out making house calls one afternoon and Juliette decided to sort through the small amount of books in the library at the back of the house. The room was situated above the kitchens and was pleasantly warm, perfect for lazy afternoon reading on chilly, rainy days. The comforting scent of stew bubbling away made her stomach grumble embarrassingly loudly. Still, she settled in and began organizing the books by subject, pausing numerous times to peruse a page or two. She'd likely make more impact if she tackled Ian's office, but she'd already decided to leave the cacophony alone lest she disrupt whatever madcap organization standard Ian possessed.

She was lost in a bit of poetry when there was a knock at the door. She could hear Mrs. Brown below her singing to herself as she worked and doubted she'd heard the knock. Juliette sat there a moment in indecision until the knock came again.

Ian had made it very clear that she was not to answer the door when she was home alone because all sorts of people came 'round to see him and request his services. He did not discriminate, so his clients ranged from dukes to doxies and everyone in between.

She'd also never answered a front door before, and the thought of doing so herself made her almost giddy. Besides, the caller was at the main entrance and not the office door; surely only a caller of quality would come that way? The last thing she wanted was for Ian to lose a client simply because she couldn't be independent enough to open the door of her own home. All she had to do was answer it, advise the caller that her husband was out, and let them know when she thought he might return.

Juliette made her decision and stood, shaking the wrinkles from her skirts as she strode to the front of the house. Straightening her spine, she opened the door…and her heart stopped.

Ethan stood on the step before her, looking hale and hearty and handsome. A pink scar from his head injury sliced through his temple and disappeared into his hairline, but Ian had done a brilliant job with his sutures. The wound had healed cleanly and smoothly.

The siblings said nothing for several heartbeats, drinking in the sight of the other person with whom they'd spent nearly every day of their existence. These last months had been the longest they'd spent apart, let alone without speaking. And it had been a special kind of torture.

Of course, Juliette was undeniably happy in her marriage with Ian, but a part of her felt lost and forgotten like a cherished toy left behind at the park. Without Ethan, something integral to who she was had been dimmed and, no matter how hard she'd tried, she hadn't been able to completely ignore it. Her throat was clogged thick with emotions, so she was grateful when Ethan was the first to speak.

"I heard you'd returned to London." He gave a weighty pause. "I waited before calling because I wanted to give you time to settle in… and I had to figure out what to say…" There was a flicker in Ethan's blue eyes she couldn't quite read, but she saw in his posture that he was trying to be stronger than he felt.

"Come in," she said softly and opened the door to admit her brother into her new home. She wiped her damp palms on her skirts as she showed him to the newly furnished parlor. The sofa and pair of chairs were placed just so before the hearth, though she had yet to purchase a carpet or any artwork to hang upon the walls. Ethan didn't seem to notice.

"I want to apologize," her brother began so suddenly that she started. She was also shocked into silence: Earls didn't apologize. Ethan didn't apologize. "I made a grave mistake in trying to stifle you, Jules; I only wanted to keep you safe. You are—" His voice broke a little and Juliette felt it like a needle in her soul; "You have always been the most important person to me."

She tried to follow it with a bit of levity and said, "It sounds like you will need a new hobby because I am Ian's problem now."

One side of Ethan's mouth lifted in a begrudging smile before he continued. "It was just the two of us for so long that I didn't know what to do. But now…now I see that I would much rather lose you to a marriage in which you seem so pleased—because you do appear happy and healthy—than lose you forever over stubbornness."

Juliette closed the space between them and wrapped her arms around her brother. When he enfolded her as well, it felt as if that missing piece had finally been returned. Tears poured unchecked down her cheeks.

"Thank you for saying that. I'm sorry, too, for running off. I've missed you so, Ethan."

He squeezed her tighter before sitting back and holding her at arm's length. "You look like Mother." She gave him a wobbly smile in gratitude. They'd both always agreed that their mother had been one of the most beautiful women in England. "Now, where is your husband?"

"Ian is working, catching up on house calls," she replied, wiping at the tear tracks on her cheeks. "Would you like me to pour some tea? He should be home for luncheon within the hour." Her smile matched her brother's.

"My, but how domestic you've become. It suits you."

Ian entered his home and was immediately greeted by the scent of fresh butter shortbread and the soft murmur of conversation from the parlor. Juliette appeared to be entertaining someone. His lips lifted in a smile. He would be lying if he said he hadn't been concerned that Juliette might not be welcomed by any of her former friends and confidants after news of their elopement became common knowledge. He was beginning to receive a handful of inquiries into the truth of the situation, but he had plenty of practice sidestepping personal questions from those in his care. He knew, however, there was nothing he could do if and when the gossip rags sunk their teeth into this juicy bit of scandal.

After setting aside his bag and hanging his coat, Ian decided to see who had come to call. His good mood evaporated instantaneously as soon as he caught sight of the familiar dark-haired man sitting beside Juliette on the sofa. Ian's every muscle tensed, prepared for the physical altercation he'd been anticipating for months now. Two pairs of remarkably similar blue eyes turned upon Ian's entry.

"Ian," Juliette greeted him warmly, her eyes dancing with the unmasked joy that always made his heart soar. She rose and immediately went to his side. Ian's eyes never left Hopesend's face. The younger man watched their exchange, his expression admirably unreadable. It took everything in Ian not to demand to know why the earl had infiltrated his home, and that he was mad if he believed Ian would ever relinquish his wife.

Finally, the earl stood and greeted him with a simple, "McCullom." Ian only nodded and waited for more from Juliette's brother. "I came to offer my gratitude in person. I've been advised several times over that your actions saved my life." His dark eyes turned to Juliette at

Ian's side. "And for my sister…thank you for making her incandescently happy." Ian's heart nearly stopped in shock. This was certainly the last thing he'd ever expected. "This is why I intend to bestow upon you the full dowry to which she is entitled." Juliette's small gasp beside Ian mirrored his internal emotions. He had no idea of what that number might be—it was certainly something that had never crossed his mind—but he had a suspicion it might make their lives vastly more comfortable. Indeed, he nearly choked on his own tongue when the earl continued. "Twenty thousand pounds, plus an annual stipend of another three thousand, in case you were wondering."

Juliette's fingers dug into Ian's forearm. He knew precisely what she was thinking: The amount was astounding and it would allow them to live without fear that Ian would need to continue to work at his breakneck pace for the rest of his days. They could reach their goal of expanding his practice; they would be able to travel and bring his experience to others.

"Your dream," Juliette whispered while looking up into his face with her tear-glazed eyes. Ian's throat grew tight. Yes, his dream had always been to help those who needed it most…but this woman before him…she was his dream as well as his reality, a new facet of his future he'd never dared to contemplate.

"Well, then…" The earl cleared his throat and approached them, holding out his hand to Ian in a peace offering. Ian returned the firm handclasp with one of his own. "Take care of her," he added in a low tone.

Ian met his piercing gaze unflinchingly, "Always."

As soon as the door closed behind her brother, Juliette threw her arms around Ian's neck and pulled him down into a deep kiss. His arms wove their way around her and he spun her in a wide circle.

Their future was wide and boundless, and he couldn't wait to share it with this remarkable woman in his arms.

Did you enjoy Ian and Juliette's story?
Look for my new spicy novella releasing in October
2024 as part of the "Curves & Cravats" anthology:
When the Duke Comes to Play...

Follow Kelsey for updates:

Instagram - @authorkelseyswanson
Facebook - Author Kelsey Swanson

Acknowledgments

I heard from so many readers that they loved Ian and were crushed when he had his heart broken in <u>Saving the Viscount</u>. Honestly, I was, too! There was something special about him and he needed his own Happily Ever After. This book was my apology to Ian for putting him through so much with Meredith. Congratulations on your love story, Ian!

As someone who had part of her childhood dimmed due to illness, Juliette holds a special place in my heart. I believe her story is one of strength and determination. She managed to find fulfillment in the hand she'd been dealt, but that didn't mean she had to settle…she just needed someone to show her the way.

Thank you to my boys for making my life so special. This past year has been another doozy, but we have persevered. Life doesn't always turn out the way we hope or plan, but knowing you both will be there to catch me gives me the strength to continue. You make me laugh and smile even when it feels impossible. You give me hope when I feel lost. I love you both to the moon and back.

I am extremely grateful to my Beta Readers, ARC group, and Street Team for helping make this book what it is.

And thank you to my amazing readers. You have followed me on my writing and publishing journey for more than one-and-a-half years now, and I hope you will continue to do so as time goes on. Your comments inspire me to write even when I am struggling. Your faith in me lights a fire in my soul to share my world and my characters. Thank you to every single one of you who has bought, read, shared, commented, reviewed, rated, and helped me along the way. I could not do this without you. And I hope you continue to follow me as I officially embark upon my future with Dragonblade Publishing in 2025!

ABOUT THE AUTHOR

Author, wife, mother, animal lover, and owner of an obscenely large To-Be-Read book stash; Kelsey is an Illinois native. She fostered her love of reading and writing after a heart condition sidelined her childhood. Her passions continued to develop long after surgery restored her health. To this day, it's difficult to find her without a book in her hands. She dove headfirst into the romance genre (perhaps) a bit earlier than the recommended minimum age and became rather adept at disguising her reading material. Once exposed to the glittering world of historical romance, she was forever changed. Her love of writing and all things British translated into her future collegiate studies in both English (with an emphasis on Brit Lit) and History (mainly British and European). She would go on to earn Bachelor's Degrees in both English and History, as well as a Master's Degree in English. She finished penning her first novel fresh out of high school and has never looked back. When she's not reading or writing, she's usually watching reruns of her favorite shows, streaming just about any true crime show; obsessively collecting architectural designs, crafts, and recipes on Pinterest; or sketching, crocheting, cooking, and spending time with her family. She is a diehard supporter of the Oxford Comma and is glued to the TV whenever le Tour de France is on.

Kelsey loves to hear from readers! Find her on social media, or email her at authorkelseyswanson@yahoo.com. Reviews on Amazon and Goodreads are always appreciated!